SICK

Amulet Books
New York

TOM LEVEEN

SICK

Library of Congress Cataloging-in-Publication Data

Leveen, Tom.
Sick / by Tom Leveen.
pages cm
Summary: "Brian and his friends are not part of the cool crowd. They're the misfits, the troublemakers—the ones who jump their high school's electrified fence to skip school regularly. So when the virus breaks out, they're the only ones with a chance of surviving" — Provided by publisher.
ISBN 978-1-4197-0805-3 (hardback)
[1. Virus diseases—Fiction. 2. Survival—Fiction. 3. Best friends—Fiction. 4. Friendship—Fiction. 5. Horror stories.] I. Title.
PZ7.L57235Sic 2013
[Fic]—dc23
2013012056

Text copyright © 2013 Tom Leveen
Book design by Robyn Ng

Printed and bound in U.S.A.
10 9 8 7 6 5 4 3 2 1

Amulet Books are available at special discounts when purchased in quantity for premiums and promotions as well as fundraising or educational use. Special editions can also be created to specification. For details, contact specialsales@abramsbooks.com or the address below.

THE ART OF BOOKS SINCE 1949
115 West 18th Street
New York, NY 10011
www.abramsbooks.com

For Scarlett

Tuesday, November 12
11:04 a.m.

"HEY, BRIAN!"

I turn to face a stout, broad-shouldered dude sporting a short blue Mohawk.

"You goin' to fourth hour?" he growls.

"Not anymore!" I say.

Chad Boris grins. It's a rare expression for him, making him appear savage. "Excellent," he says. "Jack's waitin' by the car."

I let go of the doorknob to my American history classroom and slap hands with him. We pivot and jog toward the stairs. Chad spits carelessly over the railing running the length of the second-floor walkway. Someone below shouts, "*Oh, gross!*" and Chad laughs maniacally. We hit the stairwell, run down to the ground floor, and head to the central sidewalk.

Chad stalks through the other students, pulling his shoulders back and looking menacing at anyone who gets in his way. We pass a cluster of thumb-dick football players in matching jerseys, busy sneering and smirking at all who walk by. When Chad and I go past, they pretend not to notice us at all. Such is the myth of Chad.

We're at the northern end of campus, which is anchored by the gym. Chad and I head south, past the D and C buildings. The southern edge of campus ends at the performing arts department. South of the performing arts building is the student parking lot. The campus takes up an entire block, maybe more. That's how far we're going to have to move in five minutes to get to Chad's car before the fourth-hour bell.

We're passing the B buildings when our first obstacles to freedom appear. Girls.

One wears blue jeans and a green hoodie, her chestnut hair pulled back into a ponytail—looking very cute, I have to say. Even her bubble-gum pink backpack appears vintage rather than lame, and her purple Vans are a sweet touch. The *other* girl wears skinny black jeans, a black tank, and a maroon long-sleeved overshirt. Not so cute—we look too much alike. My sister, Mackenzie, has the same dirty blond hair I do, except she's been growing hers out for about six years, whereas mine amounts to a bristle brush.

"Oh, man," Chad whispers, which is what he says anytime Kenzie appears in his line of vision.

Kenzie is scowling, not surprisingly, as she and my ex-girlfriend Laura—the cute one—walk up to us. We stop. Other students adjust course to walk around us. No one wants to bump into Chad.

"Brian, hey!" Laura says. Fairly chipper.

"Hey," I say back, avoiding her eyes.

Chad shrugs inside his leather jacket to get it to fall just right in case Kenzie is checking him out. She's not. She's examining the crimson polish on her fingernails to show us what a good time she's not having standing here with her older brother, the asshole who allegedly broke Laura Fitzgerald's heart.

"What's up, Kenzie?" Chad says. He tugs on a smile, disfiguring his face.

Kenzie shrugs. Chad tries hard not to pout.

Laura smiles up at me, which makes me feel like I've been gut shot. "So where are you guys headed?" she asks me, moving her head to try to catch my gaze.

"Um . . . American history?" I say.

"History is in the D buildings," Laura says. "*These* are the B buildings."

"And this is the roof!" I say, pointing up to the blue aluminum awning overhead. The roof runs the entire length of the main sidewalk, ending at the performing arts department. "This is the sky . . . the sidewalk . . . the bodily funk of freshmen . . ."

"Smart-ass," Laura says. Dating or not, she has to call me this at least once a day.

"Dude," Chad whispers, because the first warning bell goes off. We have four minutes to make it to the parking lot and off campus before security comes chasing after us.

Laura looks all disappointed at me. "How many classes have you missed?"

"Um . . . like, two?"

"Six," Kenzie says, giving me a sassy look.

"Six?" Laura says. "Brian . . ."

"Thank you *so* much, Mack," I tell my sister.

Kenzie, the delicate flower, swears and shoves a hand into my sternum, knocking my breath out for one heartbeat. She hates when I call her Mack. Chad laughs, then cuts himself off, like he's not sure it'll score points with her.

I rub my chest where Kenzie tagged me and face Laura. She's

still smiling in that cute way of hers. I can't help but smile back at her when I notice her eyes are brighter than they usually are at school. Like, lively.

Maybe I *am* an asshole after all.

"It would be dumb to get dropped, wouldn't it?" Laura says, kicking at my shoe. "I thought you had an A."

"Yeah, I'm acing it, but come on, babe," I say. "It's so awesome outside, we can't be locked up all day."

The hallways of Phoenix Metro High School—also known as PMS, if you're a comedian like Jack—are exposed, not enclosed, since we rarely have any weather besides *freaking hot* or *pretty nice out.* The roof over the sidewalk protects us from the sun more than from the rain—never mind snow, which is a geographic impossibility. Right now, an hour before lunch, there's not a cloud in the sky and the autumn sun is too far away to bake us like usual. Hard to enjoy the weather from inside a classroom, though.

And . . . I just called my ex-girlfriend "babe." Laura doesn't seem to notice.

"You wanna come with?" Chad asks Kenzie. "Plenty of room in the Draggin' Wagon."

Laura tugs on Kenzie's shirt. "Some of us want a higher GPA," she informs Chad.

"Don't drag me into your private hell," Kenzie sasses, and they both laugh. Oddly, Laura's comes fast. Usually, it takes a second or two for her laughs to really kick in.

"Oh, come *on*," Chad groans.

So Laura kicks him in the shin. Any dude tried that, he'd get wrapped into a tiny little ball and slam-dunked. Laura does it and it's cute. Plus Chad's wearing jeans and combat boots, so it can't hurt too bad.

Chad scowls at her, because he has to, and rubs his shin. "Friggin' ow!" he says. Kenzie laughs again, and a brief smile flashes across Chad's face. He refuses to cuss in front of girls in general, but especially Kenz.

"This is your fault," Laura tells him. "If it wasn't for you, Brian would be in class right now."

"Not necessarily," I say. "I might've jumped the fence by the tennis courts with Hollis, or maybe Jack . . ."

"Cammy told me Hollis is out sick today," Laura says. Cammy is Hollis's girlfriend, this super-athletic chick who is captain of our cheerleading squad, and I'm pretty sure the first African American girl to hold the position. We don't hold the cheerleading thing against her. She's cool.

"So, before you go breaking a law or something," Laura says to me as Chad alternates his gaze between the freedom beyond the school fence and my sister.

"Yeah?" I say.

"I was . . . Do you think we could get together sometime soon? Like, maybe tonight? Just for a bit."

Kenzie and Chad raise their eyebrows in tandem. I guess they heard the same question I did: *Can we get back together?*

"It's just that I've got something kind of exciting to tell you," Laura says.

6

"Why can't you tell me now?" I ask, trying to straddle the line between cool and cautious.

"Because we're standing in the middle of a crowded school sidewalk?"

The second warning bell goes off. Two minutes left. After that, if we're not in a classroom or with a hall pass, we get marched to the Trap, which is what they call it when they make you sit in the cafeteria and do nothing until next period. Not even homework. Freaking high school, man.

"Why don't you come with us?" I say to Laura. "We can talk at Chad's. Come on. You could use the break, huh?"

Laura lifts her shoulder up to her chin. Freaking adorable.

"Well, thanks for asking, but no."

"Chad'll drive slow," I promise.

Chad nods seriously, apparently spurred by the idea that if Laura goes, Kenzie might too. "Totally!" he says. "Ten miles under the limit. C'mon, come with us!"

But Laura shakes her head. "I've got a quiz," she says. "Maybe next time. For once."

Before I can stop myself, I squeeze her hand, gazing into her sunny brown eyes. Maybe it's that I'm having second thoughts, but I'm more bummed about her decision to stay than I normally would be.

"All right," I say. "Well . . . call me tonight, then."

Laura starts to move away. She still hangs on to my hand, though. "Thanks. I'll see you at the assembly, okay?"

"Whoa—the what?"

Laura stops. "Assembly. The pep rally? Sixth and seventh periods?"

"Ah, hell, there's no way. Mrs. Golab will kick my ass if I skip stagecraft."

"But—but it's an excused absence!" Laura says a bit wildly. Her breath starts to get shallow, and her hand tightens around mine.

Crap. Here we go. I guess nothing's changed after all.

Laura's got this panic disorder thing, like anxiety attacks multiplied by *nuclear*. Our group—Chad, Hollis, Jack, Cammy, and of course Kenzie—knows about Laura's issues, and they know she takes meds. But they don't know she's got Klonopin and Paxil in her bag at all times. She could put down a horse for a nice long nap.

She really does need the pills to keep her emotions at a level resembling normal. Problem is, they suppress *everything*. She's on the Paxil twice a day, plus the Klonopin she can take for panic attacks. Together, they damn near knock her out. She's not even allowed to drive. When she's on them, her eyes tend to be sort of half-closed, and when she laughs, it's always a second behind anyone else. But she's not like that right now.

"Hate to agree with a Brillo pad, but Brian's right, Laura," Kenzie says. "Golab is kind of a freak about missing class. And she hates assemblies. Big-time."

Laura makes these gasping noises, like it's hard to get air into her lungs. Automatically, I pull her close and hug her like

I have so many times before. I miss hugging her, to be honest, but less so when she's melting down. Doesn't exactly make for warm fuzzies.

"Shh," I whisper. "It's okay. Don't lose it."

"But I was going to try," Laura says, and I feel her starting to tremble in my arms. "I was really going to t-t-try to go and face it, but . . ."

Laura's okay out in the open air like this, and mostly okay in a classroom. But crowds any bigger than that tend to flip her out. So do driving fast, freeways, and new places. She's never been to an assembly; she always just went to the nurse or went to class. Assemblies aren't mandatory, so some teachers, like Golab, have class as usual.

"You can still go," I say. I can hardly believe she's even considering going to the assembly, but if she does, maybe that would mean she's getting a handle on things. "You'll be all right. Kenzie'll go with you."

"Totally," Kenzie says, putting a hand on Laura's shoulder. "We can go and give it a try, and if you don't like it, we'll leave. Okay?"

"Yeah, you're tough," Chad pipes up. "You can do it."

Laura shudders once before pulling away and straightening her shoulders. She struggles to smile confidently, but it fades at the edges as she says, "Yeah, you're right. I can do this."

Foot traffic picks up as we near the final bell for fourth hour. A tall blond kid, Travis, walks past. Kenzie smiles and waves at him. Travis is this big-shot actor in the drama department, and

Kenzie's taking drama this year, so I think she's required by law to have a crush on him.

"Hi, Travis!" Kenzie says.

"Hi, Mackenzie," Travis says with an easy smile.

"Hi, juice box," Chad says after him.

We share our seventh-hour stagecraft class with Travis, and Chad is not exactly his best bud. I'd explain what "juice box" means, but it's pretty gross, even by our loose standards.

Travis flips Chad off without breaking stride. Chad looks pleased with that result. The thought of Kenzie liking anyone besides him, particularly Travis, must piss him off. He doesn't have much to worry about. Travis isn't a fan of the ladies.

Right then, Frank, the most feared security officer on campus—mostly because of the bright red polyester pants he wears every day—turns a corner not more than fifty feet from us.

"That's it, c'mon, dude," Chad says to me.

"You better go," Laura says.

"Kenzie?" Chad says hopefully.

Kenzie eyes Laura. Laura shakes her head; Kenzie scowls and folds her arms. Chad looks defeated.

"Hey!" Frank shouts. "You kids get to class. Hustle up!"

"Wanna see something fun?" Chad says to us.

Before we can respond, Chad pulls on a terrified expression and runs over to Frank. "That kid has a knife!" he shouts. "He just threatened to stick me, man. That tall kid with the blond hair, he's got a knife!"

Frank immediately switches to Terminator mode and beelines for poor Travis, who doesn't even see him coming.

Kenzie bursts into laughter, which clearly makes Chad's day. I turn to Laura. "Have a good one. Bye, *Mack*!"

Kenzie flips me off with one pale hand, crimson nail polish glaring, but she grins too.

"I'll call you tonight," Laura says, touching my arm. Her fingers are like freaking *silk*, no joke. I can't help but admire her rear as she jogs down the hall toward her class. *Man.* Why does everything have to be so complicated?

Watching her go, I wonder if she'll really be able to pull off going to the assembly. If she does, that would be *huge*.

I also wonder what she wants to talk about. And why I'm looking forward to it.

I watch till she's out of sight before turning to Chad, who's enjoying watching a crowd gather around Travis while Frank searches his backpack. PMHS is allowed to search our stuff at any time, for any reason. Talk about bullshit. I've never seen an athlete's bag searched, know what I mean? Although, in all fairness, until today I never saw a drama geek's bag searched, either.

The last bell rings, and the sidewalk empties. Chad and I run past the library, the admin office, and the cafeteria. The main sidewalk ends at the back of the performing arts department, where it splits in two: east or west.

I shove Chad to the west; it's a slightly shorter path to the parking lot. We race past the industrial gray loading dock door that opens to the auditorium scene shop. The parking lot stretches in front of the performing arts building, about a hundred yards square. Freedom is a football field's length away.

I spot Chad's battered gray station wagon about halfway between the arts building and the parking lot gate. Dropping low, we snake around several rows of cars and discover Jack hiding behind Chad's wagon.

"Gate's open," Jack says, his green eyes dancing. "We can make it in the car this time!"

He means we won't have to jump the fence and walk. The three of us scramble into the car, me in shotgun.

"Security!" I tell Chad. Across the lot, another security guard, Bill, trundles toward us in a golf cart. Bill is older than God.

"He's headed for the gate!" Jack says.

Jack's right; the gate securing the parking lot is open, and Bill's on his way to shut it. It's the only way into and out of the school, and usually it's closed and locked during school hours, so Bill must've opened it for a teacher or someone. If we miss the opening, we'll be stuck.

"Go go go!" Jack screams, more for effect than anything.

Chad grunts and slams his boot against the accelerator, his Mohawk catching the midmorning sunlight. The wagon fishtails. We shoot through the gate, skid a bit on Scarlet Avenue . . . then we're free.

I look back at the school. Bill stops at the gate, shaking his head. He limps out of his cart and throws the switch to shut the gate. It rolls to a close, and Bill locks it, imprisoning all who are inside.

Jack pumps both fists. "Yes!" he shouts. "Jailbreak, free and clear."

A lot of people say their school is like a prison, but Jack's not kidding about ours. The entire campus is surrounded by a seven-foot iron fence with spikes at the top—as in, the ends are flattened into diamond shapes that can tear up a pair of jeans. The fence is painted white, to make it less imposing, I guess, but the fact is if you don't have a pass and the gate is closed, your ass is trapped inside. Unless, like us, you're used to jumping the fence.

Most people aren't used to it. Definitely not the girls. Just saying.

The three of us, plus Hollis, have climbed the fence many times, especially during lunch freshman and sophomore years, before anyone had a vehicle. But you have to be slow and careful about it, because if you slip, you just might impale yourself on one of those spikes. I've seen pictures on the Internet of some thief who literally tore his own head off trying to jump a fence like ours. Well, screw that. Lunch at Taco Hell isn't worth it. If you take your time and don't rush, it's pretty easy to climb, though.

Early in our freshman year, two juniors were killed in a car wreck right where the gate is now, back when it was an open campus. Several editorials and complaints by parents later, the whole school got locked down. To "protect us." Nobody factored in that keeping two thousand teenagers locked in one place all day is an excellent way to shorten tempers.

Violence has increased every year at PMHS since the fence went up. Sophomore year, we had a *riot*. No exaggeration. That's how we ended up with the bag-search rule. The school did a good job covering it up in the news, calling it an "altercation," but I was there; it happened. Three kids ended up in the hospital, four expelled, ten suspended. Chad was one of those ten, suspended for "instigating student disharmony." How'd he do that? He was watching the fights. How do *I* know that? I was standing right beside him. But I didn't have a blue Mohawk, so nothing happened to me. And nothing happened to the swim team pricks who were beating the almighty shit out of some stoners. I watched the swim coach pulling his boys out of the mess so they wouldn't get busted. Everyone else who actually started or took part in the riot got away clear.

So, no, I don't feel at all guilty for ditching that cesspool. We're seniors, and as such, we are expected to know better. Somehow . . . we don't. School's over in, what, six months? College, the military, working for the old man—wherever life is going to take us come summer, there doesn't seem to be much point in being super-responsible until absolutely necessary.

"Aw, man, that was killer," Jack says, stretching into his seat. "Where are we going?"

"My place," Chad says as we cross Twenty-Eighth Street, past the southeast corner of campus. "We got food."

"Excellent," Jack says. "I'm in the mood for anything whose instructions include the phrase 'Until golden brown.'"

"Golden Brown," I say. "That could be your rap star name."

And we all laugh like the idiots we are. Ditching kicks ass.

My phone vibrates in my pocket. I pull it out and see Mom's number. I almost answer it before realizing she must be calling to leave a message. She knows I should be in class. So I let it ring and put it back in my pocket. I'm hoping Mom will get me an iPhone for Christmas, because my phone sucks. Just texts and calls. The hell's the point?

Chad thumps his thumbs on the steering wheel. "Wish Kenzie woulda come," he grunts.

"Dude," I say. "For one, she's a sophomore. For two, that's my *sister*, man."

"So what if she's a sophomore?" Chad says, skipping right over the whole sister thing. "She's sixteen. She'll be seventeen by the time me'n you graduate."

"Because she missed a year."

Chad manages to both roll his eyes and nod grudgingly. He knows.

"Plus you're shipping out come June anyway," I add.

It comes out a lot more dickish than I meant. Chad's the kind of guy who's either going to wind up in jail or become a cop. Partly, I'm glad he joined the Marines, because it suits him. But he'll be gone four years. And probably going to war, the way things stand. So what if I'm going to California? I can come home, see my family. And by family, I mean Chad, Hollis,

Cammy—plus Kenzie and Mom, of course. Everyone. I don't think Chad will exactly get a lot of spring breaks in the Corps.

Chad shoots me a narrow glare, and I turn away.

"I just mean you wouldn't have a lot of time with her," I say.

"I hear ya," Chad says. "I'll miss you too, ya cockgobbler. So what was all that with Laura, huh?"

I appreciate the topic change, but not the new topic.

"I don't know," I say. "Did she seem different to you?"

"Yeah," Chad goes. "Like, not quite so out of it. You gonna hang with her tonight?"

"Probably."

"You're getting back together?" Jack says, draping his arms and chin over the bench seat. "Hell, yeah. If I was you, I'd bend that woman backwards."

"I'm going to hacksaw your face off in a second," I tell him. He laughs.

"That ain't why you broke up, though, right?" Chad demands. "'Cause of the sex thing?"

"That was never it," I say. "I didn't end it over sex."

"Or lack thereof," Jack says.

"Shut up."

"What?" Jack says. "She wasn't doing it, right?"

I shake my head, more *at* Jack than as an answer. The reality is, Laura's pills have side effects, lots of them, one of which is "decreased sex drive." Yeah, tell me about it. We got together and stuff, but not as often as I wanted. I mean, she's *hot*. I can't help that. But that wasn't why I broke up with her.

"It ain't her fault, you know," Chad says.

"I *know* it's not her fault," I say. "But dude, we didn't go anywhere. We always had to be at her house or mine. I mean, even when I talked her into going to a movie, it *had* to be during the day, at *this* certain theater, and the movie had to have been out for a long time so there wouldn't be a big crowd . . . just on and on. She'd do everything in her power to avoid having an attack. *That* was the problem. It's exhausting. I know it's a legit issue, no question, but she never tried to get better at dealing. She just never worked hard enough at it."

"Oh, yeah? How hard did you work to help her?"

"What do you think I'm doing right now?" I say. "Look, I know it sounds like I'm this egotistical asscrack who thinks he craps golden rainbows. But maybe *not* being with her will be what helps. You know? If she has to make it on her own, maybe that'll do something. Like the assembly. You think she'd be going if we were still together?"

"So you're helping her by ditching her," Jack says.

"I'm not ditching her," I say. "I don't ditch people. Not unless they ditch me first."

"How long were you together? Like, a year and a half?" Chad says.

"Just about."

"That's five years of marriage in high school time," Jack notes.

"See, that's what I'm sayin'," Chad goes. "You had all this time with her. I'd take from now till summer with Mackenzie, no problem."

Ah. So that's where all this was really headed. Should've known.

"Dude, you don't need my *permission* to ask Kenzie out," I say.

"Yeah, he does," Jack argues. "It's not like you're gonna let Kenzie put out for him, right?"

"Jack, do you hear yourself when you talk?"

"Eh. I tune in and out."

I whip my left hand up so it catches Jack's nose. He yelps and falls back. Chad laughs. Jack cusses me out; I cuss him out.

Still rubbing his nose, Jack says, "Hey, you hear about the fight this morning?"

"What fight?" Chad goes, perking up.

"Couple of guys in first period, in the gym," Jack says. "I heard they, like, went to *town* on each other. I hear some stoner dude got a finger bit off!"

"No way, man," I say. "Something like that happened, we'd know it. It'd be all over school. News travels fast. It's viral."

"Prolly just a shove match," Chad says. "But it ain't that hard to bite off a finger."

"Personal experience talking there?" I ask.

Jack laughs, but Chad just glares. So I punch him hard on the shoulder, which doesn't amount to much through his leather. Chad cheers at the inherent permission I've just given him, and belts me one back. Which I *do* feel.

Still. Beats being in school.

11:36 a.m.

WE'RE STOPPED AT A RED LIGHT ABOUT A BLOCK

from Chad's street when he suddenly gives an intense look to our left, then our right.

"It seem dead out here to you guys?" he says.

Jack and I sort of look around.

"Guess so," Jack says. "Not much traffic today."

It's almost lunchtime, and there are a lot of office buildings and stuff down this way. Usually, ditching fourth hour, we'd have to add ten minutes to the drive for traffic, but today it's almost deserted.

"Hey, if it gets us more time away from school, let's ride that pony," I say.

We get to Chad's and climb out. His mom's working, so we have the place to ourselves. It's just the two of them, and the house is kind of small, but Chad keeps the front yard looking good for his mom. The grass practically shines, and grapevines curl up along white trellises near the driveway.

Chad nukes a few pizzas for us, and we take them up to the roof with some other snacks. We go up to the roof only because we *can*. You know. Cooler. Different. Plus the weather is great.

"Hey!" Jack says, pointing to the box of cookies I'm eating out of. "That's Brian's rap name. Nilla Wafah!"

I gesture to Chad's saltines. "So Chad's name is . . . Salty Cracka."

We all laugh like total dorks. Jack starts to list off various foods we could use to nickname ourselves. Twinkie da Kid, Apple Fillin, and Chocolate Puddin top the list.

Still giggling idiotically, we're starting to crumple up our trash when a little white Toyota pickup sputters around the corner and stops by the curb. We shout at Hollis as he climbs slowly out of the truck. He does not shout back.

Hollis saved up for that car for years because he hated getting up at ass o'clock in the morning to catch a city bus to PMHS. South High School, in his part of town, closed a few years back, and now half the students from there come up here. Hollis calls the pickup "Whitey," which we think is pretty funny. I always wonder how cheer captain Cammy feels being seen in a beat-up old truck, but I'd never ask. My guess is the girls on the team, most of whom are white—or, in some cases, *orange*—are smart enough to not give her grief about her boyfriend's car.

"What the hell's up with him?" Jack says as Hollis shuffles up the lawn.

"Cammy told Laura he was out sick, but I don't know with what," I say.

I didn't know a black kid could be pale, but Hollis *is*. He walks toward the carport, his hands shaking beside his hips, his whole torso bent and stooped over in the shape of a C.

"What's up, ninjas?" he calls weakly.

Me, Chad, and Jack jump off the roof. Sweat rolls off Hollis in rivers. He's wearing a blue T-shirt, and a white bandage is wrapped around one wrist. He scratches absently at it.

"Dude . . . what the *hell*, man?" Chad asks.

"Dunno," Hollis grunts. "Caught something. Mom's got it too. People at work. It's going around, I guess."

"Why'd you bring it here?" Chad demands. "Damn, dude! I don't wanna be gettin' all sick!"

"Naw, man," Hollis says. "It's not like that."

"Hell's it like?" Jack says. "Because you look like crap, Holl."

"Dunno," Hollis says again, and tries to straighten his posture. The effort makes him wince, and he gives up. "Some kinda flu, something. Back's killing me, man."

"You should seriously get checked out," I tell him. "Jack's right, you look terrible."

"Yeah, tried that," Hollis says. "Urgent care was all backed up, and the ER woulda taken hours. So I skipped it. Saw the Draggin' Wagon, thought I'd stop by, you know."

He coughs big, whooping barks and pulls his shirt away from his neck like it's choking him. Something on his skin catches in the sunlight and sparkles. Sweat, I assume. But it doesn't look quite like sweat.

"Where are you headed?"

"School," Hollis says, wincing.

"What? Why?"

Hollis smirks sickly. "Gotta see my girl do her thing sixth and seventh at the rally. Promised her. Had to get out the house anyway. Let my sister take care of Kyle. She's feeling okay."

He coughs again, a thick, disgusting sound that makes my nose wrinkle. He sounds like a lifelong smoker about to die from emphysema. The cough is so strong it pulls Hollis several feet away from us, his hands gripping his back like the effort makes his spine hurt. He spits something yellow onto the lawn.

"Man, seriously," I say. "Go to the doctor. No kidding."

The coughing fit subsides, and Hollis rubs his chest. I think I hear something crackle under his shirt. Some kind of necklace, I guess. Maybe that's what I saw glimmering on his chest.

"Dude, Holl, I'm sorry," Jack goes as Hollis gets his breath back.

Hollis only nods painfully.

"When did it start?" I ask.

"This morning."

"How's your mom?"

"Sick," Hollis says. "Real bad."

"Worse than you?"

"Maybe. Yeah. She went to work, though. 'Course."

"Maybe you should call someone," Jack says. "I mean, if it's the whole family, and if your mom's worse than you—"

Hollis waves him off. "She'll be okay," he says. "You know how she is. Don't wanna make a fuss. Workaholic." He tries to laugh but coughs instead. He scratches at the bandage again.

I point to his wrist. "What's up with that?"

"Aw, man," Hollis whines. "Kyle. Bit me during breakfast."

"*Bit* you?" Jack goes, and laughs. "What's he, like, a vampire now? Is he pale and stylish and painfully handsome?"

Hollis grins wearily, looking down at the bandage. "Naw. He's all sick too, right, and Ma told me to take his temperature before she left for work, and bitch bit my arm. He was going all kindsa crazy, man."

"That sucks," I say. Kyle's only seven. Cool little kid.

"Yeah," Hollis says. "Well, I better go. Gotta check in with the man before they'll let me on campus, I guess."

"Hey, you know I love Cammy," Chad says, "but get your ass to the doctor. Cammy'll understand."

"Naw, I want to see her, it's all good," Hollis says. "Make me feel better, maybe."

"Well, fuck Principal Winsor, dude," Jack says. "You don't need to check in with anyone just to go to a pep rally."

"I'm blackety-black, son," Hollis says with a pained smile. "Winsor doesn't want me scaring all the whiteys without a pass."

The rest of us laugh. I wouldn't say that Principal Winsor is a racist, but Hollis is right. The black and Latino kids who *aren't* athletes don't exactly get four-star treatment at our school. It's such crap. Rumor is, Winsor was pissed when South High closed and we got a bunch of new students like Hollis, and he's been looking for a new job ever since.

"I'll see you all later," Hollis says. "Peace."

"Feel better, man," I call as Hollis climbs slowly back into Whitey. His chin nearly touches the top of the steering wheel, he's so hunched over.

Just as Hollis turns the corner, I hear three pops in the distance, like *pok pok pok*.

The three of us freeze and tilt our heads.

"Was that a gun?" Jack says, looking at Chad.

Chad squints at nothing. "Maybe," he says. "Handgun."

"Probably firecrackers," I say. "Unless we're missing a sweet bank rob—"

Two more noises cut me off, bigger bangs that echo: *KA-shoom, KA-shoom.*

"*That* was a shotgun," Chad announces. "No doubt about it."

We wander into the street, even though the sounds were way too far away to be anything happening within eyesight. Chad's neighborhood is pretty safe, far as I know. I wouldn't be surprised to hear gunshots where Cammy and Hollis live, but not out here.

We wait around a few more minutes but don't hear anything else. I shrug, and my friends shrug back at me. We go into the house and Chad flips on the TV. It's tuned to local news.

"And coming up," this plastic Barbie news anchor says, "disturbances at several area hospitals bring out the police in force." They cut to a shot of Phoenix Memorial Hospital. "We'll take you live to—"

Chad flicks the remote, and a game show comes on.

"That's where Hollis's mom works," I say. It's not far from my mom's office, about ten miles from school. Hollis's mom does medical coding or something.

"*Jeopardy!*?" Jack goes, confused.

"No, man, Phoenix Memorial."

I get a text from Kenzie just then. I check the time; the

lunch bell must've just rung at school. Kenzie sends me a few of these friendly messages pretty much every day:

You suck. :)

I text back: *Thanks Mack!!! :)*

She writes: *Ha ha. You at chads?*

Me: *Yep.* And then I remember to check my messages. Mom's left one. I call my voice mail.

"Hi, sweetie, it's Mom," she says, like I didn't know that. "Listen, I need you and Mackenzie to handle dinner tonight, okay? I got called out of town, and I don't think I'll make it back till late. Please do not have a bunch of people over, all right? See you later. Love you."

"Handle dinner" is usually code for "order pizza." Nice. I text Kenzie back with this information, then text Laura, asking if she wants to come over to share. This might work out for the best, Mom not being home. The three of us can have the house to ourselves, and I can find out what it is Laura wants to talk about.

And I hope I'm right, that she wants to ask about getting back together. I know, I know—school's practically over and I'm going out of town *and* I'm the one who ended it. But still. Even though we've been talking and stuff since we broke up, I miss her.

Laura writes back: *Pizza sounds good. Thanks.*

How you doing? I text.

Nervous. But okay. Thank you.

I start to reply when my phone goes off. Mom. This time I answer. It's lunchtime, so I'm in the clear.

"Howdy," I say, and move toward Chad's kitchen for some privacy.

"Heeeey, sexy!" Jack calls after me, making obnoxious kissing sounds, assuming it's Laura on the other end of the call.

"Jack says hi, *Mom*."

Jack's face falls. Chad curls into a ball and laughs his ass off.

"Hey, Brian," Mom says as I take a seat in the kitchen. "Tell Jack next time he's over to bring his mother's peanut blossom cookies, or I'll have Miguel do a live autopsy on him."

I laugh. Can't help it; Mom cracks me up sometimes. Her sense of humor has gotten progressively grosser over the years, probably because of her job.

"Did you get my message, sweetie?"

Ugh. *Sweetie.* "Yeah, no problem."

"Well, it's a bit more complicated now," Mom says.

I hear people in the background shouting at each other. Very weird. Mom's a doctor, working for the county medical examiner as an investigator. It's always quiet in her office.

"What's up?" I ask.

Mom sighs. "We got called out of town, some little place called . . . Arroyo? It's between here and Tucson. Miguel says there's a good chance we'll be staying overnight."

"Oh. Bummer."

"So if you and Mackenzie would—*yes, Miguel, I'm packing up now!*"

I wince as Mom shouts at her boss. "Mom? What's going on?"

"I don't know, Brian. Some emergency," Mom says, grunting. I imagine her pulling her big leather satchel over her shoulder. "There was some kind of incident at Phoenix Memorial earlier. A patient transported there from Arroyo went crazy, and Miguel says there may be more. We need to find out if some kind of outbreak has started there."

Outbreak. The word is jagged and hard in my ears.

"So what's up?" I ask her.

"I really don't know, honey. Probably a meth addict just went nuts."

"Yeah, but we heard there were problems at a bunch of hospitals."

"It looks that—*yes, Miguel, I'm coming!*—it looks that way. Listen, I need to go. Please don't have Chad or, you know, *Laura* or anyone over tonight, all right? Just you and your sister."

Damn.

"Yeah, okay. Is it cool if I head over to Lau—"

"Sweetie, I have to go."

"Um, okay." And for some reason, I add, "Be careful."

"Thanks. You too, sweetie. Bye."

I say good-bye and hang up. I go back into the living room, where Chad and Jack are shouting answers at a *Jeopardy!* contestant.

"Hey, take it back to the news," I tell Chad.

Chad glances at me. I can only guess what my expression is, because he changes the channel right away.

"—appears that federal investigators *are* on scene," a

reporter, this Asian chick, is saying in that reporter singsong voice. Behind her, Phoenix Memorial Hospital is surrounded by cop cars, lights flashing. Nearby, a bunch of dudes in dark suits talk next to a black SUV.

"Now, we don't have *confirmation* of a federal presence. That was reported to us by an eyewitness who was trying to get into the *emergency* room just a few moments ago. But the ER has been *blocked off* by police at this time. Patients are being asked to go to *other* local hospitals and urgent care clinics, but we are hearing *reports* of disturbances breaking out at these locations as *well*."

The screen splits, one half staying on the reporter, the other showing the Barbie news anchor in the studio.

"Dana, is there any indication of why the FBI is involved?" Barbie asks.

"We can't say for *certain* that that's the case right now," Dana the reporter says. "We have not *seen* or *heard* specifically that the FBI is here. We do know a *vehicle* bearing Centers for Disease Control insignia was seen *nearby*, but whether that is connected to the events *inside*, we don't know."

"What events?" Jack asks her, like she can answer. I tell him to shut up.

"Dana, is there any reason to suspect an attack of some kind?" Barbie asks. "Is this a terrorist action?"

Chad leans forward on the couch, resting his elbows on his knees. His face gets grave.

"That does not *appear* to be the case, as reports coming in *so far* give no indication of that," Dana says. "As you can see, we've been quarantined . . . excuse me, we've been *cordoned off* a ways from the building, and police have been *unable* to answer many questions."

Outbreak, a voice whispers in my head. *Outbreak.*

"Quarantined?" I say, kind of to myself. "That was a hell of a Freudian slip."

Chad nods. Jack pops a potato chip into his mouth.

"All right, thank you, Dana," Barbie says. The screen shifts to the studio. "Dana Mei reporting live from Phoenix Memorial Hospital. We'll keep you updated as more information becomes available." She shuffles some papers on the desk. "In world news, the president canceled his trip to Israel earlier today, earning a strongly worded reproach from Israeli—"

Chad hits the mute button. "Dude," is all he says.

"You think Hollis's mom's okay?" Jack asks.

"Who knows," I say. "My mom said something was happening but that it might just be a meth freak. I wonder if Hollis even knows this is going down. Whatever it is."

"Goddam terrorists," Chad grumbles.

"They didn't say that," I remind him. "We'd know if it was. It's probably just some cracked-out guy going nuts with a scalpel or something. A shove match, like in the gym."

"Or some dude got his finger bit off," Jack says, all melodramatic.

Chad shakes his head. "Naw, no way. Just one dude? He'd get dropped, guarantee it. Nurses and doctors deal with that shit all the time, especially in that part of town. It's something else."

"Maybe someone's got a hostage," Jack says with a shrug. He dumps chip crumbs from the bag into his hand and tosses them into his mouth.

"Yeah, maybe," Chad says, flipping back to the game show. "I just can't wait to get out there and do some damage, that's all I'm sayin'. Creep into *their* backyards, see how *they* like it."

Jack nods his agreement. I shake my head. It's pointless to remind Chad again that the news said it wasn't terrorists.

Chad isn't interested in any of the Marine specialties or jobs or whatever. He wants to be infantry, a rifleman, first and always. I told him *every* Marine gets rifle and combat training, no matter what job they have, but Chad doesn't care. Wherever the action is, he said, he wants to be there.

So you're ready to kill someone? I asked him when he signed up, just as pissed then as I am now.

If that's what it takes, he said back.

No way could I do something like that. I'm glad there are people who can, and will—it's not that. I just can't imagine killing another human being. I already watched Kenzie come within inches of checking out seven years ago. That was as close to death as I ever want to get.

1:02 p.m.

BY THE TIME LUNCH IS OVER, THE THREE OF US
say the hell with it and decide to skip fifth and sixth hours too. My phone rings just about the time the bell must be going off at the end of fifth hour.

"Hey, Laura-licious," I say when I answer it, then wince; her pet name came out reflexively.

"Hey," Laura says. Her voice is a little high, a little breathy. "So, are you coming to the rally?"

"Doesn't look that way. How about you?"

Laura audibly swallows. "Yes," she says, and I can hear how hard it is for her to say the word with any semblance of confidence. "I'm meeting Kenzie outside the gym. Are you sure you won't come, Brian?"

See, this is where things are hard for me. Part of me—the selfish prick side—can't help but think, *I don't have to put up with this needy crap. I could be with someone who doesn't come with so much baggage.*

But the tone of her voice, the spooked look she gets in her eyes, the way her hands start to shake . . . I want to protect her. I want to be my own civilian version of a Marine and stand up to anything that threatens her. Even if there's nothing *actually* threatening her—even if it's all in her head—it feels good to be wanted, to puff out my chest and act all badass when really I'm not.

That part of being with her, the manly-man part, includes helping her with what she needs, not what she wants. What she wants is for me to be there; what she needs is to learn how to handle difficult situations. In my opinion.

"You can do it," I say. "You'll be totally safe. I really think this'll be good for you. And you'll have Kenzie. She's a tough old broad."

I like to think Laura smiles at that, but of course I can't tell.

"Did you take anything?" I ask.

"No."

"Really!" It comes out a lot more shocked than I intended, but I *am* surprised.

"I mean, I will if I need to," Laura says. "I've got everything in my bag."

"Well, yeah, if you need to," I say, still trying to absorb her decision. Honestly, she usually takes the Klonopin like it comes out of a Pez dispenser. "Look, just keep your eyes on Cammy, relax, and enjoy it. Okay?"

She takes a deep breath. "Okay," she says, but her voice shakes. "I'll try. Brian?"

"Yeah."

"I know what you're trying to do."

"What's that?"

"Help me."

Oddly, I kind of feel choked up when she says that. "Maybe just a bit."

"Thank you."

"Anytime."

Laura takes another breath. I can hear the foot traffic surrounding her on the sidewalk, people shouting and cussing at one another.

"There's Kenzie," she says. "I'm going to go. See you later?"

"Definitely."

"I . . ." Laura hesitates. More shouts echo through her end of the phone.

"Yeah?" I say after a second.

"Never mind," Laura says. "See you later."

"Later."

I hang up and turn my attention back to an old episode of *Justice League*. Or rather, try to.

"How's she doin'?" Chad goes.

"She'll be all right." And I think, *I really, really hope she'll be all right.*

1:39 p.m.

"WELL, STAGECRAFT NEXT," CHAD SAYS TO ME, checking the time. "You wanna go or what?"

Jack's got English last period, but me and Chad are together in stagecraft, which is sort of a blow-off class in the drama department. We're supposed to be learning about lighting design, building sets, that kind of thing. Mostly, we end up painting, moving platforms, or scraping tape off the stage. It's like the drama teacher, Mrs. Golab, created the class specifically to force non-drama geeks to do all the grunt work while her technicians and performers get to do all the cool stuff.

I don't mind. It's easy enough, and we get to screw around quite a bit because Golab spends most of the period in her office while her favorite students—the techies—boss the rest of us around.

"Might as well go," I say. "Keep the easy A."

If you show up, don't bug Mrs. Golab, and don't bitch too much, you get an A and an arts credit. It's a good way to end the day. Don't get me wrong—I didn't get into Cal by slacking off, and there's nothing slacker about working in the auditorium. But it's muscle work, not biochem.

"Cool," Chad says, and turns off the TV. Jack looks a little disappointed but doesn't say anything as we head outside to pile into the Draggin' Wagon.

We pause as a rapid *whup-whup-whup* sound passes above us. All three of us look up, shading our eyes against the sun as a police helicopter swoops past.

"Whoa!" Jack shouts, and ducks like the helicopter is going

to land on him. Then he climbs into the backseat and shuts his door. "Man, they were hauling ass. Get to the choppah! Mooove! Go!" he shouts through the window in his best Schwarzenegger voice, which doesn't amount to much.

Chad shrugs it off and gets behind the wheel. I start to open my door but hesitate when I hear sirens in the distance. The sirens—fire trucks, I'm pretty sure—are headed away from us, in the direction of the gunshots we heard earlier. If they're responding to a shooting, they're doing a shitty job of it; the gunshots were hours ago. They're probably going to a car accident or something.

I get into the Draggin' Wagon and we head back to school. We gave Chad's car this dubious name after stuffing twelve people into it once for a lunch run. The rear bumper scraped the pavement as we pulled out of the parking lot.

We don't make it even a block down Scarlet Ave before I hear sirens again.

"Officers of the law!" Jack shouts at Chad, looking out the rear window.

He's right. A cop car is bearing down on us something fierce. Chad swears, slows down, and veers off to the side of the road. "I wasn't speeding!" he says to us.

But once Chad's off the road, the cop slams on the gas and roars past us.

"Whoa," Jack says to the cop car, as if the cop could hear him. "Easy there, boss."

We snicker, and Chad gets us back on the road. About a

block from school, we have to pull over again as two ambulances race past, sirens wailing.

"Damn!" Chad goes. "We missin' somethin' or what?" He picks up speed to make it back to school in time for seventh hour.

Cop cars, ambulances, the police helicopter . . . the gunshots earlier, all the stuff on the news about Phoenix Memorial . . .

Outbreak. Outbreak.

I suddenly really want to know what's happening in that little town Mom was headed to, so I call her cell, wondering if this is how Laura feels all day: sort of jumpy and nervous.

I get Mom's voice mail and hang up without leaving a message. I know it's probably nothing, but, man, it seems like it's been a weird day so far.

Chad drives past the parking lot to see if the gate is open. No luck. Muttering, he turns around and parks on a residential street across from the lot, perpendicular to Scarlet.

We walk across Scarlet and climb carefully over the tall iron fence. Basically, you have to pull yourself up and get a foot on the top crossbar, push up off that foot until you're squatting above those damn spikes, and leap from there. No big deal if you take your time.

There's no sign of security. They're probably congregating around the gym for the pep rally to make sure everyone's behaving. Just to be on the safe side, we sink low and sneak through rows of cars until we reach the sidewalk in front of the auditorium box office doors.

Chad pauses when we reach the sidewalk and looks back over the lot. "Hey," he says, "is that Whitey?"

I look where he's pointing. Yeah, it's Whitey all right, parked in one corner of the lot.

"Man, Hollis should *not* still be here after the way he was looking," I say.

"Maybe they're bustin' him for somethin'."

"Like what?"

"Bein' black."

"Right, good point."

The three of us shake our heads. You can see it on a lot of the teachers' faces, like they're afraid anyone with skin darker than bleach is going to knife them or something.

"Not like he could go to the hospital anyway," Jack says.

"Yeah, good point," I say, and get an anxious clench in my stomach. Maybe Laura's paranoia is rubbing off on me, because I'm not liking everything that's gone down today.

Or maybe, I tell myself, *it's that you broke up with a great girl because you're a selfish prick who doesn't want to put up with her freak-outs, and the truth is, you really do want her back and you feel bad for ditching her at the assembly.*

No, I correct myself as we walk around the auditorium. It's not that. I can deal with the breakup. I've dealt with worse.

The performing arts building looms over us. When they have plays or concerts, the audience goes in through the auditorium box office, which faces the parking lot. But those doors are locked during school hours, so we have to walk around to the rear—to the main school sidewalk—to get to class.

Sixth hour hasn't gotten out yet, so it's just us and a group of football players on the sidewalk when one of the other security guards—I don't know his name—comes around a corner and sees us all. Three guesses who he walks up to.

"Lemme see your pass," he says to Chad.

The football players just keep on walking, smirking visibly, proud of their invincibility.

"What about them?" Chad asks.

"Don't worry about them, I'm talking to you. Where's your pass?"

"Jesus," Chad spits, and looks at me. "I hate this place. C'mon."

He keeps walking toward the performing arts building. Jack and I follow. So does security.

"I'm gonna write you up right now if you don't show me your pass!" he says.

"Oh, yeah?" Chad says. "Do I even go here?"

"I seen you around!"

"Yeah? What's my name? What year am I?"

Right then the bell rings. The sidewalk instantly floods with students. Laughing, Jack says, "See ya!" to me and Chad and blends into the foot traffic. Most people appear to be heading for the gym. The security guard keeps rambling on about how much trouble me and Chad are going to be in, but we just dart and swerve between students and head toward the double doors of the performing arts building, which, for reasons surpassing all understanding, are painted bright orange. The security guard gives up.

"It really shouldn't be that easy," Chad says.

"And yet . . . ," I say.

Chad opens one of the orange doors, and we walk down a short hallway dividing the music department on our left from the drama department on our right. We pass a cluster of band geeks on our way, and I can see how unthrilled they are to be headed to the assembly. I can't help but smirk. Drama and band kids are a lot happier in their native environments.

We hang a right just as my phone vibrates. I check it as we walk down the drama department hallway, passing the doorways to Golab's office and a classroom.

The text is from Laura: *You back?*

I type: *Yep. You okay?*

Been better, she writes. *But okay.*

Our stagecraft class always meets in the Black Box, which is a huge classroom painted black that Golab uses for acting classes, rehearsals, one-act plays—that kind of thing. There's an outside door to the Black Box that faces the main sidewalk, right under the awning-roof, but Golab only opens it during evening performances. The rest of the time it's closed, like the main box office doors, and locks automatically from the inside.

People file into the Black Box while Jaime Escadero, this Latino dude who's Golab's favorite techie, stands in the hall taking roll.

"'Sup, *Jay*-me?" Chad says, giving Jaime a jab to the shoulder as we walk past.

Jaime shuts his eyes, like he's counting to ten or something. "It's Hi-may, you ass factory. Hi. May."

"Well, *hi* may, or *hi* may not!"

Chad cracks himself up. No one else laughs, but Chad doesn't care. Jaime's one of those rare people, like Laura, who stand up to Chad all the time and don't get their teeth handed back to them. I think Chad respects Jaime for not backing down.

"Sorry, Jaime," I say as I pass by, pronouncing his name right. "It's the blue hair dye, makes him crazy, you know."

Jaime's lips press together, but then after a sec, he grunts a laugh. He shakes his head like a horse, his long, shiny black ponytail falling into place. "Just keep that dumb *gabacho* busy for me today, will you, Brian? I'm not in the mood."

"You got it, boss."

Jaime slaps my back and returns to his grade book, checking people in. Jaime's a good guy, mostly. As long as we don't mess up "his" auditorium, and get the work done we're supposed to, he's cool. I guess he kind of runs the department, in a way. I hear that Golab's only teaching these classes because she took an acting class once in college. She was the best they could do. Another big score for our district! So the theater club exists only because people like Jaime and that tall blond guy, Travis, make it happen.

We have no desks in the Black Box, just rows of folding

chairs. I take a seat in the middle of the second row, saying hi to Clarisse, a new friend of Kenzie's this year, who is so tiny she usually gets assigned nothing more than sweeping the floor.

In the row ahead of me, Travis is complaining to another guy, Dave, that he got stopped by security and hassled about having a knife this morning. I don't even try not to laugh, which makes them both look at me. They don't say anything, though. Not until Chad sits down beside me and kicks out his legs, banging them into Travis's chair.

"Oops," Chad says, grinning. "Sorry."

Travis slowly turns around. He's nearly six feet tall, with blue eyes and movie star looks. Which is probably why he's always the lead in the plays. All the girls love him. Which is kind of amusing, when you think about it.

"Do you mind?" Travis asks Chad. His voice is obviously one of the things making him Golab's favorite actor—I've never heard a kid with such a deep voice.

"Said I was sorry, queerbag."

"That's your best shot?" Travis says. "That's the absolute best you can come up with? Really?"

"Yeah," Chad says. "You're really a queerbag!"

"Sweetheart," Travis says in his natural Shakespearean voice, "if you open this, you're getting the whole can. Know what I mean?"

"Awesome," Chad says, and stands up. Travis does the same.

Dave starts to get up too. "Hey, hey," he says. "Can you both *not*?"

I yank hard on Chad's jacket sleeve. "Dude, Chad," I say. "Seriously."

"Hell you backin' him up for, Bri?"

"Because if you start a fight and get kicked out, I won't have anyone to make fun of in seventh hour. Come on."

Travis snorts and grins at my logic. Chad grudgingly sits down. Travis moves over a couple of seats, and Dave follows, slapping Travis's shoulder and saying, "Just six more months." They're both seniors too.

I almost apologize on Chad's behalf—which I do a lot in this class, obviously—but right then the last bell rings. We're all seated when Golab walks in with her quick, short steps. She's slightly shorter than Chad, who is the second-shortest guy in stagecraft after this pudgy kid named Damon. There are only eight dudes in the whole class. The rest are girls, and most of them are actors, not techies. The only techie girl is this chick Katrina.

"Phones," Golab orders, setting a small plastic bin down on her chair.

Everyone mutters and stomps over to the bin, dumping their phones into it. Damon, the fat kid, walks up to Golab and says, "Mrs. Golab, I must protest this policy. What if I have to order a pizza?"

Golab isn't impressed. "I think you can wait," she snaps.

"But how else can I maintain my girlish figure?" Damon asks like he really wants to know. The kid's kind of funny.

Cells are an enormous no-no during class time. But as I

reach into my pocket, my phone vibrates. I know without looking it must be Laura. Golab is distracted by Damon, so I reach down and rustle the phones, keeping mine in my pocket. As long as Golab doesn't see me checking it, she won't take it away. Once we get our assignments for the day, I can sneak off and text Laura back.

Golab starts rattling off a list of jobs to do. Me, Chad, this kid Keith, and this douchebag goth-like sophomore named John are in charge of moving the platforms off the stage and into the scene shop. They just finished up a production of *Macbeth* last weekend, and most of the set is down, but there are props to put away, costumes to clean and hang, that sort of thing. The girls—and Damon—get to do the easy stuff, of course. Jaime, Dave, and Travis only have to clean the tech booth. Total rip-off.

We trudge out of the Black Box and cross the hallway to the backstage auditorium doors.

"I hate this part," I tell our group of guys as we walk into the auditorium.

"Well, let's just give it the old college kick in the nuts," Chad says. He takes off his leather jacket and drops it carelessly on the stage as Jaime, Travis, and Dave head up the center aisle of the auditorium to the tech booth.

"Bet that three-pack of juice boxes all make out up there while we're bustin' our asses down here," Chad says, grunting as he and I lift one of the platforms. These things weigh 250 pounds apiece, easy, and are a bitch to move.

Keith and John laugh as they lift another platform. They're not techies or actors either, just a couple of slugs like us looking for easy credit. But it doesn't feel easy as we maneuver the heavy platforms into the scene shop.

"You think Jaime's gay?" Keith asks as we muscle the platforms into place. "I don't think so."

"Ask him out and see," Chad says.

"What about Dave?" John says. "I don't think he—"

"*Why* are we talking about this?" I say. "It sounds like fucking Maury Povich in here."

The four of us laugh, temporary friends united against grunt work. We set the platform down and start kicking the legs closed. When we're done, Chad and I head back toward the stage. I take a quick glance around for Golab; she's nowhere to be seen, so I check my phone.

It's a text from Laura. *Big-time fight at rally*, her text reads. *Not feeling real good but I am here!!!*

"Big fight at the pep rally," I say to Chad as we reach our next platform. I text her back: *Just breathe. You can do it! You'll be fine I promise.*

"Laura made it?" he says. "She with Kenzie? How's she holdin' up?"

"Holding," I say. "She didn't say who the fight was—"

The public address speakers squeal feedback. Principal Winsor clears his throat, and it echoes throughout the auditorium.

"*Ahem.* Um . . . faculty, staff, and students are requested to remain in their classrooms for the remainder of this period," Winsor says. "We are in a state of lockdown. Um . . . thank you."

The PA squeals off.

"Hey, hey," Chad says as we lift our next platform. "Musta been a *huge* fight."

"Guess so."

We have a lockdown drill every year, which in the drama department doesn't amount to much. The auditorium's exterior doors are all locked anyway. All Golab really has to do is lock the double orange doors leading out of the performing arts department; the job falls to her since there are no music classes seventh hour. We're supposed to all go into the Black Box and wait for the lockdown to be called off, but we never do. If Golab ever came out of her office and told us to go to the Black Box, then maybe we'd take it more seriously, but until then, Winsor's announcement doesn't exactly freak us out.

Still, I'm a little more worried about Laura being there than I would've thought I'd be. If anything happens to her at her first assembly . . . god, she'll barricade herself in her house for a year.

We truck into the shop with our platform, only to find John and Keith having a fake sword fight with props from the play, as unfazed by the lockdown order as we are. The swords clang loudly, reverberating through the shop. Chad and I both wince.

"Hey!" Chad calls. "Hemorrhoids! You wanna give us a

hand here? Your other option is I take you outside and get you pregnant."

The two dorks stop swinging and put the swords down on a prop table. They walk past us without a word and go back to get another platform.

"I love my job," Chad says, and I crack up as we kick the legs closed and stack the platform.

It takes most of the period to finish moving the platforms, by which point my arms are wiped out. Chad doesn't seem bothered, but then Chad benches over two hundred anyway.

We head into the Black Box at about five minutes to the bell. Golab clip-clops her way in behind us, carrying the phone bin. She didn't come to check on us, and like everyone else, seems unimpressed with Winsor's announcement. The rest of the class files in, and we all sit again in the folding chairs. My phone vibrates but doesn't stop; it's a call, not a text. No way to answer it right now. I let it go to voice mail.

"All right," Golab announces. "Tomorrow, we're going to need to paint—"

A piercing scream from outside cuts her off.

Golab stops talking and looks at the door leading directly from the Black Box to the sidewalk outside, the door used only for performances. We follow her gaze, like we can see through the heavy wood.

"Riot?" Travis says to no one in particular.

We all kind of snicker only because it could be true, since we did have that riot once. The idea of another one starting is just stupid enough to be possible in this backasswards school. The fact is, the black kids and the Mexican kids do *not* get along, by and large. The only white kids hurt during the riot were hurt by other white kids, as far as I know. Like those swim team fucks. It's entirely possible—and wouldn't be surprising—that a couple of opposing gangs, gathered along racial lines, have gotten into it somewhere on campus.

A couple of seconds go by. Golab starts to pick up where she left off, but then we hear more screams. Shouts. Cussing.

And a stampede.

Jaime glances at Golab, and Golab gives him a nod. When Clarisse and a couple of other girls look spooked, Dave moves to stand protectively between them and the door. Me, Chad, Jaime, Travis, and Keith hop over to the door and stand behind Jaime as he yanks it open. We all puff out our chests, ready to defend the department.

Having to defend the department is actually a big part of stagecraft class. Since there are so many screwups, losers, gangsters, stoners, and other such fine specimens here at Phoenix Metro High, and so much expensive equipment in the department, Jaime and the other drama kids have, like, a license to kill. I've seen Golab slide her key ring down the length of the hall to Jaime based on Jaime doing nothing more than shouting, "*Keys!*" This, we've learned, is a code word for "Someone is in the auditorium/shop/office who isn't supposed to be, and we need to throw them out and lock up." Then they do it. Usually, what's happened is some janitor or security guard has opened a door and then not locked it behind him, letting random students roam the department looking for goodies to take.

The campus security guards generally don't care about the performing arts building, because there's never any trouble from the drama geeks. They assume it's always quiet here. I rarely see them walking these halls. And that's probably why Golab's techies get away with literally throwing kids out of the department.

Chad takes to this security aspect of stagecraft very happily, grabbing and tossing other kids out of the auditorium when Jaime says the word. It's sort of practice for his future of taking orders and being a grunt.

So we man up and put on tough faces, ready to prevent anyone from entering Golab's beloved Black Box.

But none of us is prepared for what's going on outside.

2:55 p.m.

FREAKING ANARCHY.

From the Black Box door we can see all the way down the main sidewalk to the gym, with all the classroom and admin buildings on each side. It looks like the entire student body is running around in all directions, like they're trying to get away from something. About ten yards away, this gangster guy is skipping backward, heading toward us, but his back is to us, his arms out as he screams, "*What's up! What's up!*" to this other guy in a blue shirt who is bearing down on him. Getting ready to fight.

"Hell's all this?" Chad says, smiling a little at the prospect of combat.

The gangbanger takes a wild swing and catches the other guy square on the face. The other guy doesn't break stride. He swings at the gangbanger with one massive, clubbed hand. The fist catches the gangster on the mouth.

I hear a chilling crack as the gangbanger is spun toward us. It's his jaw, hanging loose from his skull. It's been wrenched out of its socket. Blood floods his mouth and splashes against the concrete.

"Holy *shit*!" Travis gasps.

It takes the gangbanger a second to register what's happened to him. Then his eyes open wide and he gargles on a cry of pain, reminding me of that screaming chick on the poster for Pink Floyd's *The Wall*. His jaw hangs down, flopping grotesquely against his neck.

The guy in the blue shirt reaches out, grabs the gangster,

and pulls him close to his face. There's a wet, tearing sound, and then the gangbanger spins toward us again. A fist-size hole in his throat gapes wide. He falls to the sidewalk and twitches, thick blood pooling around his head.

The guy in the blue T-shirt, mouth dripping gore, spies us and starts tearing ass toward the Black Box door.

Blue T-shirt . . .

"Hollis?"

I look at Chad. His eyes are wide, and I see him swallow hard.

I barely recognize Hollis . . . because Hollis's face has *melted.* Like fishhooks have dug into the skin under his eyes and dragged it three inches down his skull. Shards of the gangbanger's throat sway from his maw. The flesh on Hollis's arms is inflamed, his forearms and hands the size of footballs. His skin seems to . . . *glitter.* Like his chest did earlier at Chad's. His lower lip juts from his mouth, swollen and distended, past his chin, giving the impression his teeth have elongated. Something beneath his shirt, something jagged, forms sharp peaks along his collarbone and chest.

"Close the door," Keith says, choking. "Close it. Close the door. Travis? Jaime? Close the door. Oh, god, *please.*"

Jaime swings the door forward to shut and lock it. Keith leans with his back against it, panting, as Jaime backs up into the Black Box. We all look at each other.

"Did, um . . . everyone else see that?" Travis asks, running a hand across his mouth.

Yeah.

We saw it.

"*What* is going on out th—" Golab starts to say, but is cut off by someone—Hollis, probably—slamming his full weight into the Black Box door from the sidewalk. Keith jerks forward from the force. His face pinches with terror—probably imagining, as I was, the monster wanting to get in.

No—not monster. *Hollis.*

The other stagecraft students, a motley crew, get to their feet and slide hesitantly toward the hallway, away from the door. They didn't see what we did on the sidewalk, but the sound of students screaming and running outside is all they need to know. They're drama geeks, not fighters.

"*Oh, god! Help me! Please!*" someone screams outside.

"Jaime?" Golab says, putting her hands on her hips. She's not even fazed. "What in the world is happening out there?"

"That guy," Keith burbles. "That guy, he tore his *throat* out, man, he tore it *out.*"

Jaime opens his mouth to answer Mrs. Golab—then closes it. Shakes his head, ponytail shimmering. He dry heaves once. Then again.

Golab doesn't get it. She eyes Travis. "Would you please tell me what is going on?"

Travis says, "Um . . ."

And then it's over.

3:01 p.m.

THE DOOR CRASHES INWARD, CATCHING KEITH

square on the head and sending him onto his ass. Hollis bursts into the room, strings of red saliva swinging from his swollen lip, his eyes yellow and bulging.

"Holl!" Chad shouts. "What the fu—"

Keith is dazed, shaking his head, trying to get to his feet. Hollis springs, grabs Keith's left forearm in both hands, and snaps his head forward, burying his teeth in Keith's arm.

Keith releases a high-pitched wail. Panicked screams burst from the stagecraft class. People trip over each other racing to the hallway. Dave runs to the hall door, shoving kids out one after the other, eyes wide and glassy.

Chad takes a step toward Hollis, then rears back as another kid—a stoner, by the looks of him—lurches through the open door. I can see past him down the sidewalk. It's chaos, kids still running madly in all directions, screaming. Other students don't appear to be running away—they're running after people, galloping toward them on all fours, moving fast, like rabid gorillas. Sunlight catches on their skin and reflects like jewels. I see Frank the security guard in his ridiculous red pants trying to get away from a fat girl who's running on her hands and feet. A second later, a white girl in punk clothes leaps on top of him, taking him to the concrete. Even over the shouts and insanity, I hear his head crack.

What the hell?

The stoner kid, wearing a Megadeth T-shirt, his face dripping skin like Hollis's, zeroes in on Chad and leaps, baring his teeth. I'm close enough that I can smell cigarette and pot smoke on his clothes. His lower lip, puffed out like a roll of fat, hangs down his face like it's been stretched. Megadeth smashes into Chad, and I get a good look at his arm. The skin's *crystallized*, like the inside of a geode, but still the color of his flesh.

Chad lowers his shoulder and rams back into the stoner, who topples into the chairs. The stoner shakes it off quick and jumps toward one of the drama kids, who's so scared she hasn't moved. Roaring, Megadeth drops the girl with one swipe of his hand.

Chad dances on the balls of his feet, fists up, prepped for a fight. Megadeth roars again and leaps toward Clarisse, Golab's favorite actress.

Clarisse doesn't even have time to scream. Megadeth pounces on her, taking her to the ground. He cocks his head, sinks his teeth into her throat, and chews violently.

Masticating! I think crazily. *He's masticating, ha-ha, that sounds like mastur—*

Chad runs toward them and plows into Megadeth, sending him rolling away. Arterial blood jets up out of Clarisse. Her blood splatters against Chad's pant leg, the floor, her own face. A blond freshman girl, standing paralyzed nearby, grips her hair and screams.

Even over the noise, I hear a snap. A wet, brittle sound to my right. I whip around—I haven't moved since Hollis burst through the door. Hollis still grips Keith's arm, one of the bones poking through Keith's skin, gray and raw. Keith sees this and passes straight out.

Hollis—

Oh, sweet god.

Hollis lowers his head and begins to—

"Out!" Jaime screams over the noise. "Everybody out! Mrs. Golab . . . !"

With Dave urging them on, most of the stagecraft class has made it into the safety of the hallway. Golab, like me, is paralyzed, still standing by her chair, eyes wide and locked on the diminishing spurts of blood pumping out of Clarisse. Clarisse played Lady Macbeth opposite Travis. Clarisse has exited stage right, for keeps.

I can still hear Hollis—

Megadeth gets to his hands and feet, glaring at Golab. From a hunkered position, he leaps at her, aiming high. He hits her throat and takes her down. Golab lets out a terrified yelp. Chad's looking from her to Clarisse's body, back to her, to me, to Hollis.

Something shoves me and I scream. It must be Hollis, he's gonna do to me what he did to Keith, oh shit—

It's Jaime. *Ohthankyougod.*

"Go!" he shouts in my face and gives me another shove.

My feet finally unstick. I peel out toward the hallway door, making a grab for Chad's jacket sleeve as I go. Travis is skipping backward, away from the outside door, as two more disfigured students leap toward the doorway. I think I have chemistry with one of them. A skinny, sickly kid named Ryan or Rob or something.

Through the open door to the sidewalk, I see Jack barreling full steam toward the Black Box. He's on both legs. Not galloping, like Hollis. Terror twists his face as he dodges the swollen, crystallized arms of another snarling kid.

Travis yanks my collar and throws me into the drama department hall. Jaime makes a grab for Chad, who is watching Megadeth tearing into Golab's neck, yanking flesh off in crimson shards as she slaps uselessly at his face. She gurgles, like she's gone into shock. Megadeth pauses for one sickening heartbeat, then attacks her forearm. With a crack, bone stabs through a ragged hole in Golab's skin, and Megadeth bites on it, shaking his head like a mad dog.

"Come on!" Travis shouts.

Chad whips around to follow. I see Jack skidding to a halt just shy of the open Black Box door as Chad and Travis scramble backward into the hallway with the rest of us. Jaime slams the door, temporarily locking the attackers inside the theater space. And leaving Jack behind.

"That was Jack, Jack was out there, we gotta let him in," I pant.

No one listens.

In the drama department hallway, kids are running in both directions, guys swearing and looking panicked, chicks screaming, huddling in corners together. But no one's attacking anyone.

John, the idiot sophomore, says, "I'm getting out of here!" and takes off for the T intersection that leads to the double orange doors.

Some of us follow, unsure, terrified.

The double doors that open onto the sidewalk are flanked by glass. A few steps before we reach them, Jack sprints into view, headed our way. I try to put on speed to get the doors open for him.

But one of these messed-up kids gets to Jack first, tackling him and smashing him against a window.

I make eye contact with Jack for a fraction of a second. His green eyes shine terribly. He knows exactly what is happening to him.

We watch and scream and cuss as the attacker tears into Jack like a carnivorous lawn mower, shredding muscle and snapping bone, spraying crimson against the window, which is almost a relief because it helps block the view of the feeding frenzy.

Jack's arms fly up, fingers wiggling like jazz fingers or spirit hands or whatever Cammy calls them, as more blood splatters against the window and runs down. Chunks of Jack stick and take longer to slide.

Through the window, I see Principal Winsor, shuffling along a classroom building wall like an escaping convict. He's looking around wildly at the chaos and seems to be trying to gauge his chances of making it to the parking lot.

And he has a gun in one hand. A pistol.

"My god," I say. Our principal is carrying a goddam gun. *And* he's trying to escape. Alone.

Two disfigured kids spot him and lunge in his direction. Winsor shrieks and waves the pistol at the kids, like a newspaper at bad dogs. Then he runs. He makes it maybe ten steps before the two students—a football player and an emaciated white girl—tackle him to the concrete. Winsor screams, and the gun goes off several times. One bullet ricochets off the pavement, and we all instinctively hunch down.

"Holy *shit!*" someone shouts. Maybe Travis.

Jaime is with our group. He grabs me, his brown eyes enormous. "Platforms and screwguns!" he screams in my face. "Now, now, now!"

Because in this building Jaime is usually my boss, I move. We lurch back toward the drama department hallway, turn right, and sprint down the hall to the backstage auditorium doors. Jaime throws them open and leads us into the scene shop. We start hoisting those heavy platforms, two people at a time, carrying them across the stage, out to the hall, and back to the doors and windows where Jack is lying still against the glass.

As Jack's blood runs down the window, Jaime shoots screws into upended platforms that Chad, me, Dave, and the techie chick, Kat, prop up.

Chad's mouth is shut tight as he stares at the floor, pressing his back into the platform to keep it steady against the doors and windows. I see his chest compress, like he's going to puke, but he doesn't. He just narrows his eyes and presses his back harder into the platform.

The creature finishes with Jack and begins pounding on the doors. We all step cautiously back from the platforms to see if they'll hold.

They do. For now.

"Oh, yeah," Travis says to no one, breathing hard. "I made a list of things to do today, and *this* was at the top."

Jaime licks his lips. "Back into the hall," he says. "We'll lock the hallway doors. Move!"

We follow him. There's another set of doors at this end of the T intersection. Closing them will isolate the theater hallway—Golab's office, the auditorium, the scene shop, the bathrooms, and the Black Box—from the rest of the performing arts department. Jaime shoves them closed.

"Keys!" he calls, and waits.

The hall is quieter now. We all look at each other. Jaime spins around. "Keys!" he shouts again.

Travis shakes his head and tries to swallow. "Golab's gone," he says. "She was . . ."

I sit straight down in the hallway, dizzy.

Chad whirls on Travis and says, "She was fucking *eaten!*"

His words ricochet down the length of the hallway and shut up every last kid in there. All I can hear is panting, my own and the others'. And that's when I process what it was Hollis did to Keith's arm.

With Keith's bone protruding, Hollis lowered his head . . .

and began gnawing and sucking on the jagged edge of calcium.

Something smashes against the door to the Black Box—one of the mutant kids trying to bash his way into the hallway. Maybe Hollis, maybe Megadeth, maybe Ryan-Rob from chemistry. Maybe all three. We scatter uselessly for cover, all of us but Jaime.

"More platforms," he orders.

"That's a brick wall, asshole!" Chad shouts. "We can't use woodscrews to—"

"Just stack them against the door!" Jaime says, running down the hall.

Our improvised group follows him back into the auditorium and the scene shop. Two by two again, we hoist platforms into the hall, stacking one on top of another until they reach almost to the middle of the door. There's no way anyone could move two or three of them stacked up, never mind the six we end up using. It'll keep the things in the Black Box from getting to us.

It doesn't stop them from trying to bash the door open, and their howls and thumping continue to reverberate through the hallway. A couple of kids whimper.

One girl, Tara, says, "What's going on?" Her voice quivers. We all look at each other.

"I—" Jaime says, and covers his mouth to fight a retch.

We jump as the PA system blurts to life with a sharp squeal of feedback.

"Uh . . . This is . . . this is Vice Principal Brandis," the voice says, echoing weirdly through the drama hall. "We have, uh

. . . a slight . . . situation . . . Students are re-re-requested to go to their classrooms and remain there until . . . until we, uh—"

A crash echoes over his microphone, followed by a snarling, feral growl that vibrates the floor beneath us.

Then nothing.

3:17 p.m.

THE POUNDING ON THE BLACK BOX DOOR STOPS

suddenly, and all I can hear is the sound of us gasping.

Jaime leans against the wall and slides down it until his knees buckle. Some of us guys—me, Chad, Travis, the squat four-eyed kid Damon, and the girl from the front doors, Kat—circle around him and hunker down. I see Dave at the other end of the hall, holding a couple of girls, one in each arm, eyes closed. John is farther away, near the boys' bathroom at the end of the hall, pacing in tight circles. Son of a bitch didn't lift a finger to help.

"We shoulda followed the lockdown!" John cries out. "We shoulda locked the doors like we're supposed to!"

Chad lowers his head, glaring at the goth kid. "You can eat my cock or shut the fuck up. Your call."

John's cheeks billow in and out, in and out, like he's not sure whether he should keep bitching. Then he gives up, folds his arms, and goes on pacing in a circle.

"Has anyone *ever* seen or heard of anything like this?" Jaime says, staring at the floor.

We all shake our heads.

"We need help," Kat states. She's this butch-looking chick, five foot nothing and maybe ninety pounds, but she can lug stuff around with the guys, no sweat. She works hard, and I like her.

Jaime stands up and runs into Golab's office. Me, Chad, and Travis follow. Jaime picks up the phone and punches 911. Waits.

Waits.

Waits . . .

"The hell?" Chad spits. "How long does it—"

Jaime holds up a hand, then frowns and slams the phone down. "A recording," he says in disbelief. "A goddam recording."

"That's bad," Travis says. He's still panting, hands on his hips.

"Yeah, brilliant," Chad says to him. Travis scowls and looks ready to respond, but Jaime cuts him off.

"Cell phones," he says. "Try your cell phones."

We all automatically reach for our pockets, then Chad and Travis both groan. I'm the only one with a cell. Everyone else put theirs away at the top of class. Like good little students. The cells are locked up in the Black Box. Along with all our bags, backpacks—everything.

I flip open my phone and try 911. I get the recording Jaime did: *We are currently experiencing a high volume of emergency calls. Please hang up and try your call again.* I tell them this.

"Not good," Jaime says. "*Not* good."

Chad doesn't have a smart-ass comment this time.

I autodial Kenzie. Get her voice mail. I try Laura, then Mom. They all go to voice mail. God*dam* it! My heart, which hasn't stopped pummeling me since we saw Hollis on the sidewalk, kicks it up another notch. Where the hell is everyone? Are they okay, or has . . .

Then I notice I have a voice mail. Must be whoever called at the end of class. I punch in my voicemail number.

The caller ID says it's from Laura's phone.

I hear Laura briefly: "Here, take . . ."

Then Kenzie's voice. "Oh my god, Brian, this is crazy . . . This guy went ballistic right when the rally started and totally bit this kid . . . and the football team, like, totally jumped him and . . . *Oh my god!*"

I hear a couple of crunches over the receiver, and can make out people screaming and running. I hear Laura's voice crying in the background, "Mackenzie, run! Oh my god, run! Oh god . . . Kenzie, head for the—"

A metallic clang bangs on her end of the line. I can hear shouts, screaming, like a concert gone mad. With one sudden crunch, the message stops.

I wait, hoping for more.

"End of message. To replay this message, press one. To—"

I close my phone. Try to think. It sounded like Kenzie dropped Laura's phone.

Jaime calls to Kat, who obediently rushes to the doorway. She's a sophomore, like Kenzie, and has been Jaime's assistant this past year. Follows him around like a puppy.

Jaime says to her, "Ask around. See if anyone still has a cell on them, okay?"

Kat nods, all business, and goes down the hall. "Hey, hey, hey! All eyes on me. Listen up."

"We need a plan," Travis says as Kat starts hunting for a cell among the remaining—*surviving*—students. "We need a plan, like, yesterday."

Jaime nods, then shoves through us back into the hall. "Tara!" he orders.

Tara, one of Golab's actresses, looks at him and comes running. She's got long brown hair and is the type of kid who auditions for every show and ends up a spear carrier or some walk-on.

"What?" she goes.

"Need you to get on the phone, call 911."

"You didn't try that already?"

"It's a recording. They're getting a lot of calls or something. You need to sit down there and just keep dialing, okay? Can you do that?"

Tara swallows once, then nods. She races to Golab's desk and picks up the phone.

"Um . . . is anyone else worried about what I'm worried about?" Travis says.

"What?" Jaime says.

"Why they're experiencing this, uh, high volume of calls?" Travis gestures toward the Black Box. "I mean, someone had to have called the cops, during the lockdown if nothing else. Why aren't they here yet? Like, maybe whatever this is isn't just here. Maybe it's *everywhere*."

"Yeah, you're right, you're totally right," I say.

They look at me.

"The news," I say, turning to Chad. "That stuff at the hospital. Jesus, the helicopter, the ambulances, cops. The gunshots we heard this morning. Something hit the fan and hit it bad."

"What stuff? What hospital?" Jaime says.

"They didn't say for sure," I tell him. "Phoenix Memorial was locked down, surrounded by cops. Maybe the . . . CDC . . ."

Outbreak.

"What the hell are you talking about?" Jaime demands.

"Tell him," I say to Chad. "I've got to try my mom again."

Chad does his best to relate everything we heard on the news and everything we saw this morning and afternoon. I step to one side and try to call Mom—and give a shout when she answers.

"Mom!"

"Brian—ank god you're—zie?"

Goddam it. The signal is shot.

"Mom, you're breaking up! Where are you?"

"—royo," I hear her say. Her voice, what I can hear of it, is high and pinched. "Something terrible's hap—type of infectious epidem—bodies everywh—"

I fall back against the wall, holding my phone with both hands. "Mom! What about the hospital? Does it have to do with that? Because we are being totally attacked—"

"—in time. Listen to me. I need you to get Mackenzie and—"

In the background, I hear someone shout something that sounds like *oughta have none.*

"Brian, I need to—but get home immediately and lock—as you can."

"Mom, wait!"

"I love you, swee—"

The line goes dead. I damn near throw my phone on the floor.

"Well?" Chad says. He, Travis, and Jaime have surrounded me, and I didn't even notice.

"Well, what?" Jaime asks him, looking from him to me.

"My mom's a doctor," I say. "She works for the county. Medical examiner's office. She's out of town, someplace called, uh . . . Arroyo. It sounded like there was some kind of epidemic. People are dead all over the place."

Out of nowhere, I piece together what the voice probably shouted at my mom: not *oughta have none*, but *gotta live one*.

"She said I need to find my sister and get home, lock the doors. I—I think. I don't know, the signal was bad. I've got to go, you guys—I've got to find my little—"

Someone pounds on the Black Box door, startling us all. A drama kid in the hall shrieks.

Kenzie. Laura. They're out there, in the school somewhere. Out there in all that . . . carnage.

"I have to call my dad," Tara says suddenly, still seated at Golab's desk. "I have to tell him—"

Jaime points at her. "*Keep* dialing 911."

"But my dad—"

"Tara, for real. We need help first. Okay?"

Tara huffs but dials again. She's a bit of a whiner, I've

noticed. Jesus, I get so sick of people who won't do the simplest work. It's a *phone call.*

"Don't you all have Internet in here?" I ask Jaime, nodding at Golab's computer, which looks about fifty years outdated. The monitor isn't even a flat-screen. "We could send an e-mail or check the news."

"The drama department?" Travis says. "Yeah, right. We don't get anything from the school. No money, nothing. Golab has to check her e-mail in the teachers' lounge."

Had to, I correct him mentally. I squeeze my eyes shut and try to scrub the memory of her death from my mental archives.

We all jump again as someone beats on the other side of the Black Box door and groans. I wonder if it's Hollis. It sounds like someone swinging a sandbag into the door, heavy and dead.

"They're sick," I hear myself say. "Remember Hollis this morning? He looked like shit. It's some kind of infection, Mom said."

Travis and Jaime take a step back, away from me and Chad.

Chad rolls his eyes. "Oh, for shit's sake. If we were gonna get sick, wouldn't we be already?"

"I don't know," Jaime says sharply. "We don't know *what* the hell we're dealing with."

"All right, fine. I start slobbering over any of you queers, go ahead and put me down."

"Cool, happy to do that," Travis promises.

"Look, I'm sorry," I say, stepping away. "I have to find my sister."

"Whoa, whoa," Jaime says. "We just boarded those doors up. You're not going anywhere."

"I'll go through the box office then," I say, and turn for the backstage auditorium doors. The box office doors have crash bar handles, the kind that are unlocked from the inside but locked from the outside. "I'll go around the front of the building."

"That's a bad idea, man," Jaime says, moving to intercept me.

"Shut up!" I shout in his face. I push past him and fling open the auditorium doors.

I hear someone cuss, and footsteps thundering behind me as I run across the stage and down into the auditorium seats. I run as fast as I can toward the box office.

Like the orange doors, the box office double doors are flanked by windows. We can see into the parking lot perfectly. I can even see Whitey still parked in a far corner of the lot.

I get to the doors and slide to a stop. I peek through one of the windows, and the other guys crowd around behind me.

"Holy . . . ," Travis whispers.

The parking lot is a killing field.

3:25 p.m.

WE'RE A SCHOOL OF ABOUT NINETEEN HUNDRED,

give or take. Pretty big, probably too big, but our numbers swelled when South High shut down. I can't be sure, but I'd guess at least two hundred kids are out in that lot.

And many of them are on all fours. The wintry November sun catches in the multifaceted growths on their arms, the skin of their faces sliding away from the bone. All like Hollis.

At the closed gate, two cars have collided before either could try to slam through the bars. They form a V right at the center of the gate. Steam or smoke rises from their hoods. Bill's golf cart is nearby, and we can see Bill draped over the trunk of one car, pouring blood from both arms. He's not moving.

At a quick count, there are no less than thirty students, probably more, moving fast on their toes and knuckles, backs hunched, flesh sagging down their faces, arms engorged and glittering. They work solo, taking down kids trying to climb that goddam tall wrought iron fence, clubbing, ripping, tearing. Other bodies are strewn across cars or lying on the blacktop as if a sniper had dropped them in their tracks.

Twenty, maybe thirty feet away from the box office doors are two more bodies. Students. Blood spills from ragged wounds on their arms and lower legs, and flows down concrete steps toward the parking lot.

The windows flanking the doors here are thick glass. I can't hear anything, and that's a small blessing; but I can *see* the screaming. Groups of students have bunched together to try to fend off attacks, but they're outclassed by whatever these infected kids have become. A lot of the defenders are obviously from gangs, guys and girls used to street fights. They last only seconds longer than the geeky kids trying to paw their way over the fence.

One diseased kid punches through a closed car window to get at a student inside. I know in the movies tough guys do that all the time, but in real life it's pretty goddam hard to do. Not for this kid. The car rocks painfully as he reaches through the broken window and tears into the girl behind the wheel. The girl floors the gas blindly, slamming into two normal kids, who get flung into the air and crash to the blacktop like scarecrows. The car slams into the iron fence, denting it but not creating a hole. The sick kid pulls the squirming driver from the window and falls upon her.

". . . *shit*," Travis finishes.

"You're gonna need a bigger boat," Chad whispers. I'm so scared, I actually snicker. We watched *Jaws* at a pool party once in seventh grade, and I haven't been able to swim at night ever since. Frankly, I don't think Chad has, either. After what I've seen so far today, I'll never be afraid of something as dumb as a dark swimming pool ever again.

"Platforms," Jaime says, eyes unblinking as he watches the carnage unfold. "More platforms. Two-by-fours, plywood, whatever we got. We gotta board this place up. Now."

But none of us move when, through the windows, we see this Latina chick in a short, bright pink skirt running panicked toward our doors. She's pursued by this enormous gorilla of a guy wearing a Phoenix Metro football jersey. He must've been at the assembly.

The pep rally.

Kenzie. Laura. Cammy, in her cheerleader uniform, rallying our pep or pepping our rally . . .

Travis's hand falls on the crash bar that will open one of the doors, but he doesn't push the bar down. Instead he watches—we all watch—as the gorilla takes the girl's feet out from underneath her. Her face crashes to the cement, splitting a gash on her forehead. A tooth skitters across the concrete toward us, and I hear it tap against one door. A second later the dude tears a chunk of skin off the girl's shin. Even through the blood, I can see her bone. Her leg looks like a barbecued rib picked clean on a sunny summer picnic.

She screams. It's close enough to hear this time, and it makes my sack shrivel up. She tries to fight the monster off. No good. He grips her leg in both mangled, crystalline hands and smashes it down across a concrete step. Once, twice, three times, over and over. Even inside we can hear the final snap of her shin giving way.

Tibia, I think stupidly. *Your shinbone is the tibia, right?*

Kenzie. Laura. Where are you?

I can't get out this way. The Black Box is blocked off, the double doors out of the arts department are screwed shut, and to go out this door would mean . . .

We're trapped, and I don't know if my little sister or Laura is even alive.

The four of us turn away from the window. Travis takes his hand off the crash bar and looks it at like he's disgusted with his own skin. At how close he probably came to letting that freaked-out football player in here with us.

"Jaime! Nobody has—"

"*Jeezus!*" Chad shrieks, and Travis lunges toward Kat, who's walked in and scared the piss out of us. Travis hugs her to his body, putting a hand over her mouth.

Behind us, something thumps into the doors. We back off and stare at the windows as the gorilla kid throws his shoulder into one of the doors, rattling it. We don't make a sound.

Thump. *Thump.* THUMP.

"Better hurry with that lumber," Jaime whispers.

Travis lets go of Kat. Her mouth hangs open as she surveys the wreckage in the parking lot.

"No," she whispers. "Oh my god. No. What's happening?"

"Kat, we need every scrap of wood, everything we can get, out of the shop and in here to board up these windows," Jaime says. "Get me?"

Kat gives herself a shake and nods. The five of us run through the dark auditorium to the scene shop. There are only a couple of platforms left, and maneuvering them around the seating in the auditorium is a bitch. We're finally able to get them and some scrap plywood mounted over the box office lobby doors and windows. The gorilla has moved on to easier prey, one of the kids hit by the car. He feasts on the kid's throat, tearing great ghastly holes.

But I don't see the girl he attacked. Anywhere. Not sure anyone else notices. There's a bright pool of blood where she fell, but no body. Maybe she made it to cover.

We give the wood a shake and decide it's as strong as we can make it. We retreat into the auditorium and sink down in the middle aisle in a cluster. The only light we have spills from bare-bulb work lights high over the stage. The orchestra pit is like a yawning black maw. I turn away from it.

Everyone's breathing hard, wiping sweat off their foreheads.

"Okay," Jaime says after a few seconds, retying his ponytail behind him. "The shop should be secure. I don't think anything can bust through that loading dock door. We got the hallway doors and the door to the Black Box covered. We should be as safe as we're going to get. I think we should bring some more lumber up to the grid. If worst comes to worst, we can run up there and block off the stairs."

The grid is a series of long metal beams sixty feet above the stage where the counterweight system attaches to the curtains. It's only accessible by a narrow spiral staircase backstage, next to the auditorium doors that open to the hallway. If we were being chased, and could get up there fast enough and block the stairs, we might be safe if anything followed us.

Safe . . .

I pull my phone back out and check the screen. Laura's text message from the beginning of class is still waiting.

Big-time fight at rally.

"Oh, god," I whisper. She hasn't tried to contact me since the end of class. Since the attack began.

"What?" Chad grunts beside me.

My stomach turns in on itself. "Kenzie and Laura. I still have to find them, man. Somehow."

"You don't *have* to do anything," Travis says.

"Dude, my sister and my girlfriend are out there someplace, and they might be hurt!" I punch in Kenzie's number. It goes directly to voice mail. Like her phone's been turned off. Some detached fragment of my brain points out that I've just called Laura my girlfriend rather than my ex.

"Bri," Travis says, "that's real noble and whatever, but you're not going out there."

"The hell I'm not."

"He's right," Jaime says. "None of us is leaving here till someone comes and gets us out."

"Somebody must've called the cops," Kat adds. "A teacher or someone. They've got to be on their way right now, okay?"

"Right," Travis says. "We were in lockdown. That means the office had to have called the police."

I get to my feet. "Screw that. If they had, they'd have been here by now. Kenzie is my *sister*, man, and Laura's my *girlfriend*. I have to see if they're okay!"

"Did you not see what's going on out there?" Travis demands. "Think, Brian."

Chad, my good buddy Chad, stands up beside me. "I don't give one squirt what a bunch of drama queers think," he spits.

"If Bri wants out, he's gettin' out, and I'm goin' with him."

Jaime's face goes deadly calm. He and Travis and Kat stand up, opposite me and Chad.

I wait for Jaime or Travis to swing at Chad, and Chad looks like he's hoping they will. He needs a fight now, after all this; he wants something he can tackle.

Instead, Jaime just says, "That's fine. Us drama queers will be happy to toss your sorry asses outside and you can show those things what a tough guy you are."

Chad tenses. But the thing about Chad—he's a loudmouth hardcore punk, but he's not an idiot. Not stupid. A total dick at times. But not dumb.

Jaime's right. I know it; Chad knows it. We're not getting out of here till the cops come get us.

But I can't let that stop me. Other than my friends—one of whom is now dead outside the orange doors and another of whom is clearly sick as hell—all I've got is Mom and Kenzie. Dad divorced Mom when I was ten, and after what happened to Kenzie, I'll be damned if I'm letting anything else hurt my kid sister. Not so long as I'm breathing. And Laura, my god—last year she panicked in a theater during a PG-13 movie. What must she have seen this afternoon, and how badly is that scrambling her brain? Even if she's unhurt, could she recover from witnessing even half of what we have so far today?

If it was Chad or Hollis or Jack out there—I mean, alive and trapped, that is—I'd try to get to them. If it was me instead of them, they'd do the same. So Laura has issues. So what? She was part of our group, absorbed by Chad, Hollis, Cammy, and Jack. And Kenzie—I mean, Jesus . . . we picked and poked at each other all the time like any other brother and sister, but not many siblings have looked death in the eye and come out the other side together.

"Look," I tell them, "Kenzie's already been through enough life-and-death bullshit, and Laura's . . . She needs help. So either you help me find another way out of here, or I swear to god, I'll tear that lumber down myself. That's a fact."

They stare at me. Jaime slowly lifts an eyebrow, and Kat folds her arms across her nonexistent chest.

"Hate to break it to you, but it doesn't get any more life-and-death than it is out there," Travis says.

"What the fuck do you know?" I shout. "You ever watch someone dying right in front of you? Huh?"

"Whoa, what're you talking about?" Jaime says.

"Mackenzie," Chad says. "She had cancer."

My shoulders drop when I hear the word. It's something we don't talk about at home anymore.

Acute lymphocytic leukemia. I haven't had to say or even think those bullshit words in years, but they're burned into my brain, into my heart. She was eight when we found out. Mom nearly lost her mind. I think being a doctor herself, being able to detach somewhat, was the only thing that kept her focused.

I shake my head to clear it. "If there's a chance I can do something to get my sister out of here, I'm taking it. We didn't go through a year of hell together just to lose each other now. I don't know how, and I don't care, but I'm going to find her and get her out of here. Laura too."

It's quiet for a minute. First minute of silence we've had since that door crashed open in the Black Box.

"Man, I'm sorry," Jaime says finally. "I'm sorry she's sick—"

"She was. It's in remission," I say. "She beat it."

"Okay, she *was*. That's great, but all hell's breaking loose out there, and jumping into the middle of it might get you killed. Maybe them too. No offense. I'm just trying to help."

"I'm with you, Bri," Chad states. "Whatever you wanna do."

I consider the options. I have no doubt Chad and I could bust our way out of here, drama kids be damned. But taking the time to think about it now, I also know Jaime's right. I won't do Kenzie or Laura any good running out of here with guns blazing just to get mowed down like Principal Winsor. Or Jack.

"All right, I get it," I say to Jaime. "I get it. I'll stay." The words taste like rancid milk.

"You sure?" Chad growls, keeping his eyes on Travis and Jaime.

"Yeah, yeah, I'm fine. Let's just take care of the grid."

Everyone seems to take a breath, and we make our way back to the shop. While on the move, I send Laura and Kenzie texts, just in case.

In auditorium. Where are you? I love you.

And: *Are you ok?*

I close my phone and pray for a response.

"Brian," Kat says, her voice soft, "I don't want to make you mad, but . . . could I use your phone? I'd really like to call my mom."

I hand it to her. "God, yes, sorry. Go for it."

"Thanks." Kat takes the phone and walks off a bit for privacy.

I say to the guys, "If you want to call anyone . . ."

Travis thumps me on the shoulder. "That's cool, man. Thanks."

"Yeah," Jaime says. "Thanks."

"Chad?"

He nods. "Sure, I'll give her a call," he goes. "Don't matter, though. We're gettin' outta here, one way or another. I plan on bein' home by the end of the day, havin' dinner with Mom like always."

No one responds.

Kat stands with the phone in her hand, not up to her ear, gazing emptily at the stage floor.

"What's wrong?" I ask.

Kat doesn't move. "I don't know my mom's number."

"How can you not know your mom's phone number?"

"It's on my cell," Kat says. "I haven't dialed the number in over a year, when she got her new phone." She shakes her head. "I have no idea," she whispers.

God, she has a point. How many phone numbers do people actually have memorized?

I wonder how many other students would have the same issue. Without Internet, without their phones, without so much as a damn phone book, calling people may turn out to be one hell of a big problem.

Operators, of course, are "unavailable at this time." Thanks.

Chad, then Travis, and finally Jaime borrow my phone next. Chad's mom doesn't answer her cell. Travis tries to have a conversation with someone I assume is his dad, but whoever it is must be one righteous asshole, because Travis hands the phone back red-faced and pissed. I don't ask questions. Jaime manages to catch his mother at home. They speak Spanish together for more than ten minutes.

"What did she say?" I ask Jaime.

Jaime's face is dark. "She wanted to come get me," he says, handing me the phone. I check it quickly for any texts or messages. Nothing. "I told her not to try."

"Good call, for now," Kat says, hefting a stack of short two-by-fours to take up to the grid.

"But she can't reach 911, either," Jaime says. "Same message we got. She's been watching the news . . . It's bad."

We all tense visibly.

"All the hospitals are in lockdown," Jaime says. "There's attacks happening all over the city. No one knows what it is for sure. Maybe terrorists, maybe something else. She said they're waiting for the governor to declare a state of emergency."

"Well, hally-flipping-luyah," Travis says with a snort.

"She said to stay here," Jaime adds. "But Asa, my little brother . . ."

He turns away. Travis puts a hand on his shoulder.

"He goes to Madison," Jaime says through tight lips. Madison is one of the junior high schools that feed into PMHS. "She can't get through to them."

No one has anything to say.

Jaime clears his throat. "Anyway. Come on. Work to do. Let's head up to the grid."

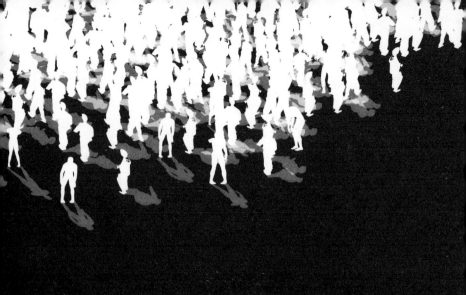

4:52 p.m.

WE SPEND ABOUT AN HOUR MOVING STUFF UP
to the grid. No one's in a hurry, even after a couple of ominous thuds echoing from the box office; I guess we're feeling fairly secure.

We finish loading up the grid with scrap lumber and other junk in case we need to escape up the stairs and barricade the steps behind us. When we're finished, we go down the spiral stairs and head for the hall. Jaime opens the door, and we're suddenly surrounded by the entire rest of the stagecraft class, everyone talking at once.

"What's going on?"

"What were you doing in there?"

"What are we gonna do?"

"Why isn't the phone working?"

Jaime shoves through them and holds up his hands. This is his class, his auditorium, his department. He's the boss now.

"Quiet, quiet, shut up," he says. "What did you say about the phone?"

"In Mrs. Golab's office," says a heavy black girl named Serena, one of the coolest chicks in the whole department, with a voice almost as deep as Travis's. "Tara was talking to her dad, and then it went dead."

We turn to Tara, who is lingering by the office door.

Tara shakes her head. "I—I . . ."

"You *what*?" I say.

"I told you to only call 911," Jaime says through a tight jaw.

"I know, but I had to talk to him . . . I lost the dial tone," Tara whispers. "It just shut off."

Jaime squeezes his eyes shut.

"What'd he tell you?" Chad demands.

Tara hugs herself and shivers. "He loves me," she says. "That was all he could say . . ."

The small crowd erupts with more questions. Jaime shakes his head and holds his hands up again.

"Shut up!" Jaime orders. "Now listen. We boarded up the box office doors, so no one's getting in or out, okay? If anything from . . . if any*one* from outside gets past that, then head up the spiral stairs to the grid. We'll create a barricade from there if we need to. But we should be okay here until help comes."

"Why can't we just leave?" Dave asks. He looks spooked, but at least he's not losing it.

No—not spooked. Something else.

"We don't want to do that," Travis says.

"Why not?"

"Because we're trapped," I say, spitting the words. "The whole school is locked in. The parking lot isn't safe, and there are cars blocking the gate, which is closed and locked anyway. There's more of those . . . people . . . sick people out there. A few dozen, maybe more. Some kids were trying to fight them off, but it wasn't working. They're strong, really strong."

"What's the matter with them?" Damon asks me. He takes off his glasses and polishes them with his shirt. "They don't like the cafeteria food, either?"

Nobody laughs, but part of me appreciates his attempt. "Man, I don't know. It's just some kind of sickness."

"Or terrorists," Chad mutters.

"So someone's coming, then," that idiot sophomore John says, sounding frantic. "The cops are coming, yeah?"

"We don't know, dude, all right?"

"So the best thing we can do is sit tight and wait for help," Jaime says. "Just . . . try to . . . try to stay calm, try to relax, and we'll take it one step at a time."

This is enough of a speech to break up the crowd. Dave, as he's stepping away with the others, puts a hand on Travis's back and mumbles something I can't quite catch. A couple of girls come up to him, and Dave leads them away, talking softly.

I take a head count as they disperse around the hallway. Twenty-two, not counting me, Chad, Jaime, Travis, or Kat. Twenty-seven all together. Damon, his glasses back on, glances at the retreating crowd, at us—then folds his arms, standing beside Travis. Joining our team, I guess. Would've been nice to have his help on the grid, but then we didn't ask for help, either.

"Weapons," Chad says. "We need weapons."

"Right," Jaime says. "The shop."

"Hold up," I say. "You mean for self-defense, right?"

"Kenzie's out there, man," Chad says. "Laura. Cammy. If you plan on busting outta here to find them, you sure as hell can't go without somethin' to swing at those things. Seen what

Hollis did to that loser Keith?" Chad jerks a thumb toward the Black Box door.

I did. Oh, god, I did. The sounds he made, chewing on Keith's arm . . .

Chad looks around and lowers his voice. I feel like the entire stagecraft class is straining to hear every word.

"Imagine him or a buncha people just like him gettin' in here," Chad says.

"Much as I hate to say it," Travis says, rubbing the back of his neck, "Mohawk here has a point."

"I wanna help our buddy Hollis out," Chad goes on, ignoring Travis. "I do, 'course I do. If there's a way to do that, awesome. But I'm not gonna bet my life on it right now. Or yours, or Kenzie's. So you call it self-defense if that makes you feel better, but we ain't gettin' caught naked. Get me?"

Slowly, I nod. I don't like it—but then there's nothing here to like.

"Right," I say. "Weapons."

"Okay," Chad says. He nods to Jaime. "Lead the way, *vato*."

Jaime clenches his teeth but turns and heads back to the scene shop door at the end of the hall.

Our group, now including Damon, walks with him. Dave is sitting against one wall, still comforting the two girls. Quite the ladies' man, I guess. But he's my size, maybe a shade bigger, even. I don't like the idea of him staying behind—he should be a part of the plan.

While the others march to the shop, I squat down beside

Dave. One of the girls, I think her name is Brandi, wears a short-sleeved shirt the same shade of maroon as Kenzie's. Just the color of it stabs my chest.

"Hey, man," I say to Dave, and the girls don't even look at me. "Not for nothing, but I wouldn't mind having your help."

Dave doesn't meet my eyes as he shakes his head back and forth. "Love to," he says. "But I can't. Clarisse and Mrs. Golab. Keith. I just stood there."

"You didn't just stand there, you got people out," I say. "Dude, *I* just stood there."

"Yeah, but . . . you won't next time." He finally looks up at me. "I could have helped Clarisse. Or Mrs. Golab. I was close enough. I just didn't. So . . . I think I'm more helpful right here at the moment." He uses his eyes to gesture to the two girls curled up beside him.

I glance over at Serena, who is doing the same thing. She and Dave—two seniors guarding kids younger and smaller than them. Hell, it looks appealing to be one of the freshmen, let someone else handle this mess.

"Yeah," I say, standing up. "Okay. I get it. Thanks."

"Brian."

"Huh?"

"Thanks for asking. If it changes . . ."

"You got it."

I head for the shop. John, that little cock who helped us tear down the platforms during class but hasn't lifted a finger since then, looks at me as I walk past. Asshole. I'll give Dave a pass because at least he's comforting people. John's by himself.

"You going to help?" I say without breaking stride.

He doesn't reply. I reach the shop door and call back over my shoulder, "Fuckin' pussy."

I don't wait for a response, and don't hear one. In the shop, I join the others and work fast. The rolling cargo door is firmly in place but occasionally bangs hollowly as something outside tries to get in. We can hear moans, growls, howling. It sounds like hell is waiting for us outside, and it's hard to tune out.

I check my phone, just in case I didn't hear it or feel it vibrate. Nothing. No calls, no texts. I fight back a high-def image of Jack being torn apart and try not to think about it happening to Laura, or about Hollis maybe being the one to do it. Could I hit one of my best friends, fully intending to hurt him badly? Maybe. If it came down to him or Kenzie—or Laura—then I'd have to. But it's Hollis. I mean . . . he's the one who introduced me to Laura, for god's sake.

Hollis, with his easy laugh and laid-back attitude, made friends with her in AP algebra sophomore year. When Hollis hooked up with Cammy, Laura ate lunch with them both in the cafeteria, and me, Chad, and Jack happened to join them. I owe Hollis a chance to find help, and I owe Laura a chance to get out of this god-awful mess.

I sit down on the shop floor, holding my head in both hands. Chad notices right away and shuffles over to me.

"What?" he goes.

"I told her to go to the rally," I say.

"You mean Laura?"

"Yeah. I told her to go, man. Jesus. I could've talked her into coming with us to your place, or just going to class. I practically forced her into going to that goddam assembly. If anything's happened to her—"

"Whoa, hold up," Chad says, squatting down in front of me. "Lookit. You were tryin' to help her, dude. Who would've thought somethin' like this could happen? Whatever the hell it is . . . C'mon, man, she's probably fine, and this ain't your fault. Cut that shit out."

"I even told Kenzie to go with her, so if something happ—"

Chad slaps his palm straight into my forehead. Not enough to knock me over, but it gets my attention.

"Hey," he barks. "We don't got time for this. Laura wanted to go, and Kenzie wanted to go with her. That's a fact. We don't know that anythin' bad happened to them. Didn't see them in the parkin' lot, right? So they're both prolly holed up with a buncha other kids in some classroom."

I lift my eyes. "I've got to find out, man."

"I'm with you, brother. Say the word, and we're off like a prom dress."

Behind Chad, several yards away, I can see Travis and Jaime hefting chunks of wood, testing them for strength and functionality as weapons.

"I don't want to hurt anyone," I say.

"You might change your mind if one of those kids gets in here. Plus we'll need something when we go looking for the girls."

I nod. Chad rises and sticks out a hand, which I grab. He hoists me up.

"Let's soldier up," he says.

We join the others in scrounging around the tool closet and prop room for weapons. When we're done, Jaime lines everything up on a folding table.

"Here's what we got," Jaime says. He picks up a sword from the production of *Macbeth*, one of the ones John and Keith had been messing around with during stagecraft. "This is a Starfire—"

"It's a fake sword," Chad blurts in disbelief.

"If you'd shut up for a second," Jaime says, and takes a breath. "It's a Starfire. It's combat-ready. These things are built to be hit again and again and again. So they're not sharp, but they're built to last."

"They're *fake* swords," Chad insists.

Jaime's lips disappear between his teeth. He turns, eyes a plaster statue of an angel a few feet behind him that was part of the *Macbeth* set, and swings the sword. The angel's head crashes off and smashes against the floor, momentarily drowning out the sounds of the damned outside. The plaster head makes the same sound Frank's skull did on the sidewalk.

Jaime points the sword tip toward Chad. "Now, how about I swing this at you and you tell me how fake it feels, *pendejo*?"

Chad grins. "I like how you think, *ese*. G'head."

I take the sword from Jaime. It weighs about five pounds, pretty heavy. The edges are totally dull, and the point isn't too sharp. It can be held one- or two-handed, with a total length of about two feet. Jaime's right—you could definitely cause some damage with it. As much as I don't want to find out, if it came down to it, I wouldn't mind having one of these in my hand.

Jaime points out a length of solid steel pipe, a baseball bat, and a couple of DeWalt screwguns. He presses the trigger on one, making it whine. "We put our longest, biggest drill bits on the screwguns," he says.

I imagine one of those bits chewing right through one of the sick kids' skulls. I wouldn't want to fight a guy who had one of these; it's a good weapon.

If you get close enough to use it.

Which, for Chad, is the main problem.

"Hold up," he says. "Don't you have any, like, guns in this place?"

"Oh, sure," Jaime says, nodding vigorously. "Oh, yeah! We got a whole arsenal in here. Sure, grenade launchers, machine guns . . . *Jesus*! Are you *insane*? Why the hell would we have guns in here?"

"Hey, someone had to bring it up," Chad says. "You'd feel like a tool if someone had a gun and no one asked."

"Anyone have a gun?" Jaime shouts with this big, sarcastic smile. "Anyone here have a . . . a . . . a nine-millimeter ceramic *Glock* they forgot to mention over the past couple hours? Huh? No? Nobody?" He turns back to Chad. "Gee, I guess not."

"I do," someone says.

We all turn to Damon. He rubs one eye beneath his glasses and clears his throat.

"You do *what*?" Jaime asks, like he's not sure he wants to know.

"Have a gun. It's not a, you know, Glock, but . . . yeah. I got one. Thirty-eight hammerless revolver with integrated grip laser sight."

Silence.

"My mom gave it to me," Damon adds, like it'll ease the creepy factor. I can't tell if he's joking.

"Well, where is it?" Kat asks him, crossing her arms over her belly like it nauseates her even to be asking the question.

"Out there. In my car. Brown two-door Honda. Under the driver's seat."

"In the parking lot," Travis says. "Which is surrounded by those—things. That doesn't help."

"I'll make a go," the fat kid says. "I'll try. If you want. I mean, check me out. Is this not the body of an Olympic-level sprinter?"

We all look at each other. I *think* we're all thinking the same thing: No way in hell. For one thing, his joke aside, Damon doesn't look like he can outrun much of anything, let alone one of those sick kids out there. Second, I don't think *any* of us have the skill to get out there, and back, in one piece.

Literally.

I smack a hand over my mouth to prevent a giggle and wonder if I might be going crazy.

"Too risky," Jaime says.

Chad whips around on him. "I'm not so sure you get to make that call."

"Hold on," I say. "If we thought we could make it to Damon's car, then there'd be no reason to come back here with a gun. If making it to a car in the parking lot were a real possibility, we'd be talking about getting over that fence, or trying to bust right through it, not about getting a gun. You know?"

"That girl in the parking lot," Travis says. "She tried to bust through the fence with her car. So, like, *oops* on that one." He brushes his mouth with the back of one hand.

"And in any case, we don't know how many of those freaks are out there," Jaime says. "We'd never make it. And, well, *plus*—"

"What the snap crackle fuck you talkin' about?" Chad says. "I say we keep our options open, keep an eye out. If we see a break, we take it."

"Not. Right. Now," Jaime says, gritting his teeth.

"Plus what?" I ask him.

"Huh?"

"You said 'plus,' like you had something else to say."

Jaime closes his eyes for a sec, then sits down on a ladder resting on its side, making him sit at an awkward slope. We hunker down around him on the floor.

"Yeah, that," he says, gripping the edge of the ladder as if for balance. "Look, it's . . . it's like this, okay? I didn't see any of those things out there trying to get over the fence. Did you?"

Those of us who were in the lobby shake our heads; it's true. It didn't look like the sick students could get over the fence. Their backs were too messed up, all hunched over. Based on how Hollis looked this morning, my guess is it might actually hurt them to stand straight.

"Considering how hard it is for a student to get off campus under the *best* circumstances, my feeling is those things are trapped here right now. Even if we broke a hole in the fence somehow to escape, they would too. They'd get out. And god only knows what might happen then."

"You mean we'd risk . . . I don't know, contagion or whatever?" I ask.

Jaime nods, not looking happy.

"Even if it is already spreading," he says, "we can't be a part of letting the infection out of here."

"The hell we can't," Chad says. "Whatever it is started outside the school, jackass. My buddy Hollis was sick as shit this morning, and now he's like *Day of the Living Dead* in the Black Box."

"Right," Travis says. "So you might come down with it, huh? Maybe we should lock you in the prop closet or something."

"Why don't *you* get back in the closet, ya fuckin' dildo?"

Travis tilts his head. "Do you fuck your mother with that mouth?"

Chad's face goes from white to red in two-point-three. Not a good idea to get anywhere near insulting his mom.

"*Shut! Up!*" I shout.

Travis and Chad look at me. Damon takes a step back. Kat clenches her hands.

"We can't do this. We can't *be* like this," I say. "We can't. Got it? Sad to say, *we* are among the most sane people here at the moment, and if we lose it, then everyone's toast. Okay?"

Travis takes a step back from Chad, ceding ground. Thank god.

"All right," Jaime goes, blowing out a breath as Chad glares at me. "Now, I don't want to be all Mr. Worst-Case Scenario here, but I think we better plan ahead a little. 911 and the phone not working—that's bad. If this thing, whatever this is, is already across or beyond the city, we need to prepare for the worst here."

"You think it is?" Travis asks him. "Beyond the city?"

"I think he's right," I say. "I mean, where are all the parents? If there's anyone else alive on campus, they'd have phones, they'd be calling home. This place should be crawling with adults coming to pick up their kids, and we haven't seen that. Whatever this is, it's big, and it's bad."

"Won't the Army or someone come?" Kat asks. "I mean, sooner or later? Maybe people are just quarantined away from here right now."

"Not the Army," Chad says. "National Guard, maybe. If the governor gets off her ass in time."

"Why not the Army?" Damon asks.

"Because the Army is federal," I say. "You know that hurricane, the one in New Orleans?"

"Katrina," Kat says, smirking bitterly. "We just read about it in class."

"Right, right, Katrina. One of the reasons that got so jacked up was the governor didn't let the feds in right away. We just talked about it in history. The states can't be, like, invaded by the feds. The governor can activate guard troops, but not the Army and whatever, not unless she asks for it."

"And we don't know if she's done that yet," Jaime says. "Like my mom said. They were still waiting for the order."

"Well, what's it *take*?" Damon says.

"Red tape," Chad says. "Trust me. Could take a long-ass time."

"Yeah, think about it," I say. "They have to figure out something's wrong first. Who knows how long this has been building? We know the infection isn't instant. Maybe this has been going on under their noses for days. Months, even. By the time anyone figures it out, it's too late."

Great. As if I wasn't scared pissless already, now I've succeeded in scaring myself even more. Based on the expressions of the rest of the group, they're thinking the same thing.

"How long can we stay here?" I ask, trying to change the subject to something practical.

"You mean before we start looking around for a conch shell?" Travis goes.

"I was hoping to avoid that, but yeah."

"The hell's a conch shell?" Chad demands. "Like, shells for a gun?"

"It's literature, sweetheart," Travis replies. "You wouldn't understand."

While Chad balls his hands into fists, Damon says, "Maybe people have food, you know, candy bars or something. Plus whatever is in the fridge and freezer in Mrs. Golab's office? I mean, I can eat my weight in Taco Bell each day, so we might want to look into that."

He has a point. A lot of Golab's favorite students get to keep their lunches in her office, which has a full-size side-by-side refrigerator-freezer. No way they'd step foot in the zoo that is the cafeteria at lunchtime—where the riot started two years ago—if they didn't have to.

"The water is still on," Kat says thoughtfully. "So there's running water in the bathrooms and drinking fountains."

"Right," Travis goes. "So, call it a week if we divvy up the food and ration it out. We can go a long time without eating. If the water stays on, theoretically, being the young, strapping lads we are, we could go a month. If we had to."

Damon's stomach growls, and we can't help but laugh. A very, very little.

"Look," Chad says, and I can see he's trying hard to keep his cool. "That's all great, okay? But I still think we need to keep an eye on gettin' outta here all together. Find help, whatever. I don't care how much food you all say we got, it ain't gonna last forever. No matter how bad it might be outside, at least we have room to maneuver."

Sounds like a Marine already.

Travis and Jaime look at each other, then Jaime nods. "Okay, that's fair. You're right." He looks at the rolling door, which has fallen silent. "All right. We need more information. Let's head up to the roof. We're in the tallest building on campus—we can get a better idea of what's happening outside from up there. Maybe we'll get lucky and they'll just start dropping. Or fighting each other."

"You mean like a normal school day?" I ask. That earns me a few grudging smirks.

We follow Jaime into the auditorium. On the way out of the shop, I hear Chad's voice low behind me saying to Travis, "You talk like that to me again, and I'll cut your nuts off, you get me?"

Travis laughs. "Honey, I heard you, but I can't make myself care."

"Fuck you, man."

"I'd be bored; you'd fall in love." Travis pushes past me to catch up with Jaime and Kat. Chad moves to walk beside me, with Damon lagging behind.

"Hate that prick," Chad growls. "I'm gonna whip it out and dick-smack him so hard he'll have a mushroom-shaped bruise on his forehead. Know what I mean?"

"Hey, man," I say in a voice I've honed over the years specifically to get and keep Chad's attention without pissing him off. "I hear you, but you got to back off a bit. Cool?"

Chad snarls.

"At least Travis is helping out," I add. "Not like that shithead John."

Chad grunts an agreement. Hopefully it means he'll ease up. I sock him in the shoulder to make him feel better, then check my phone.

Still no messages. I text Kenzie again.

Please tell me you're ok.

Chad sees me do it. "Anything?"

"No."

"Laura?"

"I think her phone got dropped. In the gym."

"Sorry, man."

"She's all right," I make myself say. "I'm sure she is. Probably in a classroom or something, like you said."

God. I don't believe it. I just don't. I can hear it in my own voice. But it raises another interesting question.

"Jaime," I call, and break into a trot to catch up with him. Chad and Damon follow. "Listen, man. You know how we were just talking about other people out there?"

Jaime stops at center stage and raises an eyebrow.

"Trapped people, I mean," I tell him. "In classrooms. The offices, library. Where there's no running water, or food—"

"Maybe they're in the cafeteria, in which case they're doing a lot better than we are on that issue," Kat says.

"I don't know about that. You ever see the cafeteria food?" Damon cracks.

Jaime's not having it. "Yeah, have *you*? It's poor-kid food. Free lunch might keep you alive, but not by much. It's cheap and easy and total crap."

I imagine Damon saying, *So's your mom!* and laughing his head off. Like Jack would've. But Damon only looks away.

"Shouldn't we find out?" I ask.

"Find out *what*?" Travis says.

"Who else is out there," I say. "They might need help. Almost everyone was at the pep rally. Maybe there are people trapped in the gym."

"You've seen what happens when those things go lawn mower on you," Travis says. "We can't risk going to look for other people. We got enough problems right here as it is."

"Pansy ass," Chad mutters.

"Our pansy asses kept you alive today," Jaime says. He continues walking to the foot of the spiral staircase that leads to the grid. "Brian, I know you want to make sure your sister's okay. I get it, man. I'm worried about my parents and my little brother right now. And if there are other people trapped around campus, we'll keep an eye out for them, but the best thing we can do is sit tight, okay? Give the cops or whoever time to come get us."

"We don't know anyone's comin' to get us at all," Chad points out.

"They will," Jaime says.

He starts climbing up the stairs.

"They will," he says again.

If he'd just said it once, I'd buy it. But that second time . . . I don't think he believes it himself.

5:15 p.m.

WE CLIMB THE STAIRS AFTER JAIME. WE REACH the catwalk and step carefully across the grid. There's a ladder bolted to the wall about halfway across. Jaime goes first, throwing open the ceiling hatch, letting in graying sunlight. He jumps up and shouts, "All clear!"

Like we couldn't have guessed that. One by one we climb up after him.

The first thing we notice makes us all stop and stand still. I feel a little ball of vomit start making its way up my throat.

The smell.

And then the sounds.

They come together and assault us. Even without looking over the edge, I know below us is hell. Damp, gurgling moans creep up the walls and spill over onto the roof, like thorny vines reaching for our feet. We instinctively group closer together for a sec, then split up and head for different corners of the roof.

"Fire," Kat says from the north edge. "Downtown. Look."

I start to turn toward her, but Chad's voice stops me.

"Same here," he says.

We scan the horizon. There are three distinct smoke plumes rising over the city. Big ones. I hear fire engine sirens, but they're real far away. Way off in the distance, way too far to signal, three helicopters race toward downtown. I don't think they're news choppers. Somewhere to the west, I hear popping sounds like we heard this morning at Chad's. Gun shots.

"Did we get bombed?" Damon asks.

Jaime licks his lips. "I don't think so."

I walk to the west edge of the roof, on the side where below us the rolling door leads to the shop, and peer down to the sidewalk. My guts twist tight at what I see.

"Um, guys?" I say. "It gets worse."

They jog over to join me and look down.

"Ah, shit," Chad whispers.

It's Hollis.

And Keith.

And the girl we saw from the lobby. I recognize her bright pink skirt dotted with drops of blood.

They're shuffling along the sidewalk, backs hunched and cramped, moving like apes on their knuckles. Keith and the girl don't even seem to notice they have broken bones sticking out of their skin. Their arms reflect sunlight back at us from the crystalline formations on their inflamed skin. They wail incessantly, somewhere between weeping and pain. The crystals on their hands scrape against the concrete.

We move away from the edge, each of us a shade paler than the minute before.

"Okay," Jaime says, trying, it seems, to sound calm. "Now we know. It *is* infectious."

"Unless you're already dead," I say as a picture of Jack lying against the windows outside the department flashes in my head. No way he was getting up and walking away; his whole throat had been torn open. Keith and the girl in the skirt . . . they must not have bled to death.

Jaime peers over the edge again, his nose wrinkling. "No sign of . . ."

We know who he means. Clarisse or Mrs. Golab. Like Jack, they were almost torn to pieces from the throat down.

"If you're still alive when they're done with you, you turn into one of them," I say, choking on something dry.

"But if you're dead, you stay dead," Damon says. He takes a shuddering breath. "Is that good news or bad?"

"If it's infectious, then are you guys feeling okay?" Travis says, squinting at me and Chad.

"Been over this," Chad warns.

"No, no, it's fair," I say. "I feel all right. Chad?"

Chad, still frowning, says, "Yeah, sure, I'm tip-top. Oorah."

"For real?"

"You siding with them now?"

"I'm just asking, man. We've got to stick together. Are you feeling all right?"

Chad huffs a little, then says, "Yeah, I'm fine. Pissed and ready to beat the crap outta somethin', but otherwise fine."

"I don't think it's airborne," I say to Travis. "I think we're okay."

Travis nods, still looking suspicious. I suppose I can't blame him. "Transmitted through blood, then, I'd guess," he says. "Saliva maybe."

"When did . . . ," Kat says, then bites her lip. "How long's it been since . . ."

I guess what she's trying to say. I pull out my phone, check the time. "It's been two hours since Keith was bitten," I say. "Not quite that long for that girl."

"Fast," Damon whispers.

Chad frowns. I mean, more than usual. "But Hollis," he says. "We saw him before lunch, and he was fine. Well, not fine, but not goin' apeshit crazy, and not all deformed like that. When do you figure he, you know. Changed?"

"I don't know," I say. "Maybe there's something that speeds it up. Or slows it down."

We consider this new twist for a few moments, watching smoke rise from around the city. I wonder vaguely how the fires were caused.

"My car's just over there," Damon says finally, pointing at the parking lot.

We all look. The Honda blends in with the rest of the used cars most people have at our age, except for one notable feature.

"The one with the big-ass white peace symbol on the window?" I ask him.

Damon nods.

"Is that even a little bit ironic considering you have a gun under the seat?"

"I'm a pretty complicated gentleman," Damon says with a sick grin.

"That's a long way to run," Jaime says. "It's almost dead center in the lot. I don't like it."

"Maybe not right now," Chad says. "But let's keep our options open."

Chad's right. Of course he's right. The question is: What the hell *are* our options?

That's when my phone vibrates in my hand.

5:20 p.m.

I DAMN NEAR DROP MY PHONE. IT'S MOM.

"Yeah?" I say quickly. No time for formality.

The reception is clearer now. I sort of wish it wasn't.

Mom's crying.

"Brian," she says. "Thank god. Are you all right?"

I sit down hard on the pebbly surface of the roof. Chad and Jaime hunker beside me, while Travis, Kat, and Damon take a cautious peek over the edge again.

"I'm fine," I tell her.

"Where are you, honey?"

Glancing at Chad and Jaime, I hold my phone out and hit the speaker button. "I'm still at school," I say. "You're on speaker, okay, Mom? I'm with Chad and some people from the drama department. There's some really crazy stuff going on."

"I know, I know, sweetie," Mom says. Normally, I'd wince or laugh or groan at her calling me that when other people can hear it. But no one seems to notice.

"Tell me exactly what happened," Mom says.

So I tell her everything, starting with Hollis looking sick. It's not like I'm going to get in trouble for ditching. I describe the sick kids, what they've done so far. And that we're basically trapped.

"Dear god," Mom says when I'm done.

"Mom, what is this? What's happening?"

"Is it terrorists?" Chad says.

"Hi, Chad," Mom says, her voice weary as it sometimes gets when Chad's around the house too long. "No, we don't think so.

But something strange happened here in Arroyo. Several days ago, by the looks of it. Some kind of infection. Our preliminary findings indicate an unknown pathogen. A bacteria similar to the one found in patients with septic arthritis. Patient Zero may have been an older diabetic man suffering from gout."

"Patient Zero?" I ask.

"The first victim," Mom says. "His whole body is . . . He looks the way you described the kids at school. The sick kids. But this old man, he was . . . Someone shot him with a shotgun. The whole town, it's gone. Everyone's dead. They've been torn apart. Or else shot."

Jaime swallows hard. We all stare at my phone like we didn't hear her correctly. But of course we did. We've seen it.

"There was one survivor that we know of, a young man, but he's virtually catatonic. We haven't been able to get any information out of him."

"Why is it happening here?" I ask her. "I thought this Arroyo place was pretty far away."

We hear Mom sigh. "Based on the reports we've gotten, the current theory is that an infected person must have made it as far as Mesa or Gilbert, seeking treatment after being attacked," she says. "Then they were transferred to Phoenix Memorial, where they had more resources. But this patient may have begun behaving like the others and might have bitten several people before she ever made it to the hospital. And by then . . . Oh, god, Brian, it's an absolute disaster. Thank god you're all right."

Mom pauses.

"Where is Mackenzie?"

I try to speak. Can't.

"We'll find her," Chad says for me.

"She's not with you?" Mom cries. "I've been calling her cell phone, but she hasn't answered!"

"We'll find her," Chad repeats. "Me and Brian, we ain't gonna let anythin' hurt her, okay, Mrs. Murphy? We'll find her and we'll get her outta here."

Jaime gives me a glance that says Chad's being a little too optimistic. Well, fuck him.

"Brian, honey?"

"I'm here," I croak.

Mom clears her throat. "Listen to me," she says, trying to keep her voice steady. "I do want you to find your sister and get her home safe, or keep her there with you in the theater department if it's secure. But, Brian, you must not risk contact with the infected. It's beginning to look like the initial infection took a day or more to cause symptoms, but that time has been shortened as the bacteria mutates. Do you understand?"

I slowly get to my feet. Chad and Jaime follow, eyeing me.

"Are you . . . you want me to just leave her out there?"

"I want you to stay safe and protect yourself," Mom says. "You must not let these infected children bite you or touch you with any bodily fluid, or even breathe near you."

"So it's like the flu?" Chad says, looking worried.

"We're not sure," Mom says. I can imagine her rubbing

her forehead the way she did when she tried to explain how Kenzie's illness worked. "Blood and saliva, almost certainly. It's more challenging to pin down whether any incidental contact can spread the disease."

Chad folds his arms over his chest and grimaces.

"Either way, there's no way of knowing if we can find an antidote or treatment or vaccine, or when," Mom says. "We have to hope for the best and prepare for the worst, and I need to know that you are as safe as you can make yourself. All right?"

I don't say anything.

"Brian?"

"What are the chances of finding a cure?" I ask her, struggling against the nightmare images of Laura or my sister becoming one of those things.

"I can't put a number to it, sweetie," Mom says. "But there's always hope."

"Um, excuse me, Mrs. Murphy," Jaime says toward my phone. "I'm just curious—what *is* happening here in Phoenix? Do you know? We don't have access to the news, and 911 calls aren't going through."

"Who is this?"

"My name is Jaime Escadero, ma'am. I'm the, uh . . . stage manager."

"Jaime, it's a miracle I got through as it is," Mom says. "Cell towers have gone down all over the place. You probably know more than I do. But based on the reports we've been getting, this bacteria has spread, and spread fast. You should stay inside and wait for help. I'm sure the feds will be mobilizing soon, if they haven't already."

"So it's a state of emergency?" Jaime asks. "Declared and everything?"

Mom pauses.

"Not quite yet," she says.

We all groan.

"The hell's the holdup?" Chad demands from no one in particular.

"I'll tell my people you are all there," Mom says. "Just sit tight, please. Try not to panic, and for god's sake, don't cross paths with anyone who is sick. We'll get you out just as soon as we can. Brian?"

"Uh-huh," I say.

"I need to go. Did I make everything clear?"

"Sure, Mom."

"All right. I'll call you back just as soon as I can."

"Okay," I whisper.

"Good-bye, sweetie."

"Bye."

I click the end button, and we all stare at each other. Damon, Kat, and Travis have stopped looking over the roof edge and stand nearby. Kat sidles up next to Jaime like she's about to hold his hand.

"That bad, huh?" Travis says.

"Pretty," Jaime says, and turns to look at the parking lot.

"Anyone need to call someone again?" I ask. I suddenly don't even want to be holding my phone anymore, like it's infected.

Jaime reaches for it. "Yeah," he says. "Thanks."

But his call won't go through.

"Travis?" Jaime says, his voice hoarse.

Travis stares at the phone. I see his jaw clenching and unclenching in the fading sunlight. The rays collide with smoke from downtown, creating a dismal sunset.

"Naw," Travis says suddenly. "To hell with him. He can't wait for me to get out of the house anyway. Maybe he'll get his wish."

Kat steps to Travis and hugs him, which in a way is kind of amusing because her head hardly reaches his chest. Travis hugs her back, still glaring at my phone in Jaime's hand.

Damon quietly takes the phone from Jaime instead. Whoever he calls, though, doesn't answer. He hands the phone back to me, trying to look brave. "Maybe I'll try later, if that's okay," he says, and snaps his fingers like he just remembered something. "Still need to order that pizza."

I never really got Damon's humor. But right now, I'm kind of grateful for it. "Sure, man. Sure thing. Kat?"

She breaks away from Travis, who's folded his arms and winces out at the sunset. "I can't remember the number," Kat says. "So stupid . . ."

"Chad?"

"Mom's either fine or she's not," he says. "I'll find out eventually."

I swallow something bitter and put my phone back into my pocket.

"Might be your last chance," Jaime says, looking out at one of the smoke plumes.

Chad scowls. "I ain't givin' up, if that's what—"

"No, I mean, maybe no one should make any more calls anytime soon," Jaime says. He looks at me. "Unless you happen to have a phone charger on you."

"Ah, *shit*." He's right. The battery won't last forever. "All right, we save it for emergencies."

Which is a dumb thing to say. What exactly would constitute an emergency at this point, and who the hell could we call, anyway?

"Let's go," I say, and head for the trapdoor.

We climb back down the ladder and the stairs and into the auditorium. In the drama hallway, John comes up to us.

"What's going on?" he asks us. "Where were you guys?"

Jaime sighs. I look around the hall. The others are sitting along the walls in small groups, fidgeting nervously and watching us. It dawns on me that of everyone left in the building, this little group of ours is the only one *doing* anything.

I get the feeling we're in charge now.

I don't like it.

"Let's get everyone together," Jaime says. "We need to let them know what's going on."

Kat nods and goes up the hall, gathering the other students. They make their way over to us. Jaime hunkers down, so we all sit around him. All of us except Chad, who kicks back with one boot against the wall. Kat sits beside Jaime. That kind of makes sense; she's probably next in line to inherit Jaime's jobs when he graduates.

If any of us make it out of here.

"All right," Jaime says, exhaling. "What we know is this. Calls to 911 aren't working. We tried, but it wasn't happening. And now the office phone's dead. Right?"

Tara nods. "I keep trying, but so far . . ."

Jaime waves her off. "Some fires have broken out around town. We saw three for sure."

One chick starts crying, the blond freshman who gripped her head and screamed during the attack. Serena wraps an arm around her, whispering. For one weird second, I want her to do the same to me. Serena looks so normal, so safe.

"The other thing is . . ." Jaime stops and looks at me, Chad, Travis, and Damon. We all shrug.

"Brian?" Jaime says. "You want to take this?"

"Uh . . . sure. Well, it's some kind of sickness," I say. "A bacteria or something. The people out there, the ones who ki—who hurt Mrs. Golab and Keith and Clarisse, they're sick."

No need to say *killed*. They know. I explain the possible illnesses the sick kids have as Mom described them. Several people make disgusted faces.

"So we're gonna get sick?" John asks.

"Naw," Chad says. Everyone looks up at him. "We'd know by now."

"Chad's probably right," I say. "It looks like, um . . . it looks like . . ."

The hallway is silent. They wait for me to finish.

"Like they have to bite you," I say.

Jaws fall slowly open all around the hall.

"You mean they're zombies," that idiot John says, eyes wide.

I get a triple-speed flashback of the last four years hanging out with Hollis, and get instantly pissed. "Don't call them that," I say.

John stands up. He dresses like a douche bag vampire, his dark hair hanging in his face.

"If that's how they infect you, they sound like zombies!"

Damon adjusts his glasses. "Zombies are technically undead. These people aren't dead. They're just sick."

"What the hell would you call them, then?" John's voice is starting to get hysterical. "Somebody's chewing on your bones, they're *not* just sick!"

I get to my feet. "Dude," I say to John. "They're not zombies, okay? Cut that shit out." I'm still thinking of Hollis as I say it. No one's calling my bud *anything*, I don't care what he's done.

Then I think about the gun in Damon's car. How ready Chad was to go get it. That we've got a melee arsenal assembled in the scene shop. My *god*, what is happening to us?

"Okay, how about monsters?" John goes on.

"Don't you get it?" I shout at him. "They are people, they're people we go to school with who are sick and who might be dying!"

And, I don't bother adding, my sister and my girlfriend might be among them for all I know. My sister was sick once before, and the thought of anyone referring to her as anything other than that makes me want to hit something.

"*We're* dying!" John says. "And *they're* killing us! That makes them monsters. You think that shit is just gonna wear off? They just, what, need two aspirin and a nap? God! They're already dead, man, dead and walking. That makes them *un*dead, which makes them zombies in my book."

My hands turn into fists. "We don't know if they can be . . . *fixed*," I sputter, knowing even as I speak what a stupid word that is to use, but too pissed off to correct myself. "And *dying* is not the same as dead."

"No, but it's next-door fucking neighbors, isn't it?"

"Whoa, whoa, whoa," Chad says, holding up his hands. "Am I the frickin' peacekeeper now? Chill out."

I'm so tense by this point that I almost risk taking a swing at my best friend, if for no other reason than I know he can take it. Just to have the satisfaction of hitting something.

"Tell 'em what your mom said about that town," Chad says to me.

Everyone in the hall stares up at me, eyes wide, hungry for information. I tell them everything Mom said about Arroyo. Kids gasp and clutch each other as I explain the entire town was wiped out.

"But we saw helicopters here, downtown," I say. "Maybe it's the FBI, or CDC, or . . . CNN for all I know. My mom is telling people we're here, and they're going to come get us out."

Eventually, I think to myself, but don't say it.

My cell vibrates in my pocket right then. Without thinking, I pull the phone out and open it up. "Hello!"

"... *Brian*."

"He's got a phone?" someone whispers stupidly at my feet. *Of course I have a phone*, I want to shout. *You think my mother was up on the roof?*

I walk through the seated group, and they all rise to their feet behind me.

"Kenzie?" I say. "God, where are you, are you okay? What's happened, where are you?"

"They're still here," Kenzie whispers. "Oh, god, they're right outside. They were too close to use the phone before now. I had to shut it off so it wouldn't make any noise at all . . ."

I shut my eyes and grit my teeth. It's her sick voice, her scared voice, the voice I heard for a year while she fought through the leukemia. She sounds as young now as she did seven years ago while we waited and prayed.

"I gotta call my mom!" someone shouts behind me.

I wave my arm behind me to shut them up.

"Kenzie," I say, "listen to me. Where are you? Are you still on campus?"

"Me too!" someone else shouts. "I gotta call my family! I'm next!"

"We're in the library," Kenzie whispers. "Behind the check-out counter. But there's these . . . *people* outside . . . and the librarian, she looks like a . . ."

"No way!" another kid squeals. "My dad's sick at home. I have to call him first!"

I barely perceive sounds of a struggle now developing just a few yards behind me. I turn to look; five or six different kids are shoving each other as Chad, Jaime, and Travis try to calm them down. Serena's on her feet, clapping her hands and shouting to break it up.

"I know, I know," I say into the phone. "We're coming to get you, okay? I swear to god, I'm going to come and get you. But listen to me, Kenzie—"

"Brian, please, I'm *really* scared here."

"I know, I know, okay? But you've got to listen to me—"

Most of the remaining stagecraft class is now in a free-for-all shouting match, arguing over who gets to use my phone next. I see the two girls Dave has been consoling actually punch each other while he tries to split them up.

Jesus. It's a panic, worse than when we all evacuated into the hall from the Black Box. Worse because, for the moment, we're actually safe from those sick people and are instead swinging at each other.

Just like I'd been about to.

"Stay where you are," I say quickly into the phone. "Stay right where you are and stay quiet. And listen—don't let them bite you. Okay? Whatever you do, do not let them bite you."

"Did you say *bite*? Why would—"

"Just do it," I order her. "Okay? We'll come to get you as soon as we can."

"*I called it first. I'm calling my house!*" someone screams above the chaos.

Shit. I'm going to have to put the phone away, and fast.

"Kenzie," I say. "What about Laura? Have you seen Laura, is she with you?"

"Laura . . ." Kenzie sniffs quietly. My heart sinks. "Yeah, she's in the—"

"*Brian!*"

Chad's baritone breaks through the noise. I spin around just as some chick tackles my arm, yanking the phone away from my ear before I can hear Kenzie finish.

"Gimme it!" the chick screeches.

The phone pops out of my hand, flies through the air, and nails the opposite wall. It falls to the ground, and the battery bursts out.

This unleashes the rest of the crowd. They charge after my phone before I can even move, tangled up in this chick's hands. The phone gets kicked one way, the battery another. Feet stampeding, kids screaming for the phone, people crying.

"Break it up!" Jaime shouts, barreling into the middle of them. "*Break! It! U—*"

A cracking sound penetrates the din.

Everyone shuts up and stops moving.

"Oh, no." I groan and shove through them. "No, no, *no*, you *idiots . . .*"

They back off. My cell lies in two pieces, the screen shattered.

I bend down and pick the pieces up. Dumbly try to fit them back together at the hinge. No one says a word.

I throw my head back and scream.

The others flinch, then move quickly down the hall. I fall to the floor, holding the two pieces, one in each hand. I think I might be crying.

I chant a litany of cuss words for some time before I sense several bodies surrounding me.

"Man, this sucks," I hear Chad say above me.

"Sorry, Brian," I hear Travis say to my left.

I get to my feet and snort up a wad of snot. "This is ridiculous," I say helplessly to no one in particular. I hack the snot into my throat and spit it against the wall. "This is a goddam *clusterfuck*."

Jaime is on my right. He casts a worried look over his shoulder. I follow his gaze, ready to pounce on anyone in that group who makes one single sound.

Jaime turns back to us. "We'd better secure the food," he says quietly.

I glance down at the busted phone in my hands. Destroyed in a blind panic. Fear.

"Yeah," I say back.

"Follow me," Jaime says, and turns to face the group down the hall.

Chad, Travis, and I fall into step beside him.

We are definitely in charge now.

And I'm not waiting another second to go get my sister.

5:31 p.m.

IT'S ONLY BEEN A COUPLE OF HOURS SINCE THIS whole situation started, and already we're falling apart. The blond girl in Serena's arms is just flat-out breaking down, sobbing. John's pacing in tight circles again, muttering something about zombies. Everyone else—except for Kat, who's scowling and watching Jaime, awaiting orders—looks dazed and fearful.

My expression might have something to do with it.

Jaime leads us right through the middle of them. Kat falls in behind, with Damon behind her. Jaime marches into Golab's office, waits for us to enter, then quickly shuts the door and throws the doorknob lock. He stands with his back against it.

Kat picks up Golab's phone, listens, sets it down. "Phone's still out."

"Brian," Jaime says. "In the corner. Red bag. Look for a bike lock."

I cross to Golab's filing cabinet, where a red duffel bag sits on the floor. I unzip it, revealing a violin case, some books, and at the bottom, a thin bike chain in blue plastic with a padlock on the end.

"Chain the fridge," Jaime orders.

I don't argue. I go to the white refrigerator with side-by-side doors and wrap the chain around the fridge and freezer door handles several times, then snap the lock shut.

"There's a whole bunch of really scared people out there," Kat says. "They're going to need to be dealt with."

Something about the words she chose makes my skin crawl.

Jaime takes a cautious step away from the door, as if to make sure no one is going to try to bust through from the hall. "What are we going to tell them?" he asks us. "About the food?"

"We're not gonna be here long enough for it to matter," Chad says.

"We might be," Travis argues.

"This is the United States of America," Kat says, pretty calm under the circumstances. "We're not in Rwanda here, you guys. Someone'll show up, we've just got to sit tight."

"Naw, no," Chad says, wagging his head. "We gotta get the hell out is what we gotta do."

"Where's the key?" I ask Jaime. "To the bike lock."

Jaime pats his pockets; keys jingle. "I got it. It's safe."

Chad squints at him. "Now wait just a damn minute," he says. "Who the hell put you in charge?"

"Why does it matter?" Jaime retorts. "Thought you were getting out of here."

"Listen, you Mexican piece of sh—"

"All right, stop," I say, interrupting Chad as Jaime clamps his mouth tight. "You saw what happened to my cell. Jaime was right. We're the only ones trying to be, like, proactive here. Far as I'm concerned, those idiots in the hall can flip out all they want. Until someone in a flak vest rappels into the auditorium, we're *it*."

They look at each other. Jaime nods, relaxing ever so slightly while Chad sneers. I remind myself that we're all under stress, a metric shit-ton of it. Otherwise Chad wouldn't have said anything like that to Jaime. No way.

"Now, I won't speak for anyone else," I go on, "but I know for a fact that my sister is alive in the library. With other people, by the sound of it. So one way or another, I'm going in there to get her out. Meanwhile, you all can dickslap each other for who gets to be the Big Bad. But I got work that needs getting done."

"This is the safest place to be right now," Jaime says.

"Okay," Chad says, shrugging. "Okay. Cool. That's true. Oh, and by the way, how's your little brother holding up?"

Jaime freezes so still and complete it unnerves me. I feel my legs tense, ready to jump in between him and Chad if he goes nuts.

Instead, Jaime turns around, away from Chad. Slowly, millimeter by millimeter, the tension in his shoulders melts, until his entire body seems to sag.

"You're right," he says quietly.

"Not tryin' to be a dick," Chad says. "I'm just sayin'."

Jaime turns to me. "If you did get to your sister, then what? Try to get off campus?"

I sit down on Golab's fake leather couch and hold my head in both hands. "I hadn't gotten that far yet."

"Wait a sec," Travis says. "I thought you wanted to stay holed up in here, Jaime."

"For the most part, yeah," Jaime says. "But I also want to go get my little brother. And go *home*."

Being a teenager sucks. You're not an adult, but not really

a kid anymore. We spend most of our time pushing for all the adult stuff. Cars and money and all that. But when Jaime says *home* like that, I swear to god I drop to six years old because I understand instantly what he means.

I just want to go home too.

Chad either ignores his tone or leaps over it. "Right, gettin' off campus, yeah," he says, nodding vigorously. "So we agree? I think that's our plan. If we could find a—"

He cuts himself off and snaps his fingers. "My car, it's not in the lot!" Chad says. "It's parked outside the fence, across Scarlet. Not even a block from the parking lot. You can *see* it from there."

The others perk up. Damon says, "So if we could get past the fence . . ."

"The zombies *and* the fence," Travis says.

"Dude," I say. "Don't call them zombies, all right?"

"What kind of car?" Jaime asks.

"Station wagon. Big old huge bitch too. I've gotten twelve people in there once before. It wasn't comfy, but we did it. Realistically I'd say . . . seven to ten." He looks around at us as if taking count. "Us, anyway. That's six. Call it four more. Three with Mackenzie."

"Two left with Laura," I say.

Nobody responds. I get pissed, then scared, then ill. It's like they won't even consider her.

"Dave," Travis says quickly. "We got to bring Dave."

"That leaves one seat left," Damon says softly.

"Hey, my car, my call," Chad says to Travis. "I ain't holdin' no frickin' lottery, pal."

Travis takes a breath, ready to argue, but Jaime holds up a hand to silence him. Guess all these years of Jaime being in charge of the plays still applies, because Travis shuts up.

"Plus what about Cammy?" Chad says, looking at me. "If we can find her too, we gotta get her outta here."

He's right. We can't leave Cammy here. If she's alive. If *any* of them are . . .

Jaime paces the short distance between the door and Golab's desk.

"Maybe," he says carefully. "Maybe we can break this down, step by step, and all get out of here alive."

"I'm listening," I say. Because no matter what, my mind's made up.

"But we don't do it half-ass," Jaime says. "We get on the same page and we stay on the same page. Otherwise someone'll do something dumb and get us all killed."

"Why're you lookin' at me?" Chad says.

"Because you're reckless," Jaime says. "Questions?"

Chad glares at him. "Well! . . . Huh. No. No, not really."

"We handle the food issue first," Jaime says. "Then we talk rescue operation, recon, and escape."

"Wow," Chad says. "That kinda gives me a boner, I'm not gonna lie."

Jaime smirks. "Glad to hear it. All right. On me."

He unlocks the door.

5:40 p.m.

JOHN'S OUT THERE WAITING AS SOON AS JAIME opens the door.

"Hey, what were you guys—"

I throw a palm into the sophomore's chest, sending him backward. The crowd, which has gathered around the door, backs up. John scowls at me, and I stare him in the eye until he looks away.

"Listen up," Jaime says. "Here's the deal. One, remember the phone is dead in here. So don't anybody go stepping all over anyone to get to it. You want to see for yourself, fine, but believe me, if it was working, we'd be in there talking on it. Get it?"

Nervous nods. John rubs his chest, making a pissy face at me.

"Number two, we're talking about trying to get out of here," Jaime goes on. "But it's going to take some time and patience. What I need all of you to do is chill out. Just try your best to relax, and don't do anything stupid. Those things are still out there, so just sit tight. When we have a plan, we'll tell you."

"Who put you in charge?" John says, but stays back where I had pushed him.

Chad stalks up to John, who cowers.

"I did," Chad grunts in his face. "You got somethin' you wanna say about it, cold sore?"

I blink in shock. It's the last thing I would've expected Chad to say. Not the cold sore thing, but about Jaime being in charge.

"N-n-no," John says.

Chad nods, and turns back to Jaime, folding his arms over his chest. "G'head."

Jaime's mouth twitches into a grin, but it's gone as quick as it came. "Kat made a good point a minute ago," he says to everyone. "We're not in the middle of nowhere. We're in the sixth-largest city in the country. Somebody's going to come for us eventually. Brian's mom is telling someone we're here, and she's a cop."

Not exactly true, but I don't bother correcting him.

"The best thing we can do is wait for them, just like if we were lost somewhere."

That runs exactly counter to what Jaime said in the office, but I don't point it out. Right now, it's probably more important to get these kids to settle down than to let them in on our plan.

Whatever that plan is. That's when I realize why Chad backed up Jaime's authority: the sooner we get everyone settled down, the sooner we can figure out how to get the hell out of here.

"Meanwhile," Jaime says, wrapping up, "just be cool. All right? We'll be in the scene shop."

A dozen voices protest.

"John," Jaime adds over the noise, "you're in charge out here. Keep everyone cool. Get me?"

John's face gets serious and he nods his head. "I'm on it," he says.

My respect for Jaime Escadero skyrockets. It's a brilliant

move, and John buys into it instantly because he's too stupid not to. Now not only will someone work at keeping everybody calm, but it'll keep John out of our way. Plus I see Jaime give Dave a clandestine nod as if to say, *Make sure he doesn't screw it up.* Dave tips his head back to indicate, *No problem.*

Jaime jerks his head at us. Me, Travis, Chad, Damon, and Kat fall in behind him. Not sure what good Damon will do, but maybe Jaime's plan involves going for Damon's gun. Or maybe Damon has a girlfriend or sibling on campus he's worried about.

Or maybe, like the rest of us, he just wants out. I swear the hallway walls are inching closer together, sucking up oxygen.

We march to the shop. The last thing I hear before Damon shuts the shop door is that freshman girl crying into Serena's shoulder, echoing down the hall.

We gather around the table where Jaime's weapons are assembled.

"All right," Jaime says, resting his hands on the tabletop. "So how do we get to Chad's car?"

"We don't," I say. "Not right away. Not without my sister and Laura."

Jaime clenches his jaw again, like he's biting something back. "Right," he says at last. "But once they're safe, we start talking about how to get off campus. Cool?"

"Cool."

"You said Mackenzie's in the library, so I say we go aerial,"

Jaime says. "We can climb down from the roof of the auditorium and drop to the roof over the main sidewalk. Follow that to the north. It's maybe fifty, sixty yards to the library."

"We won't be able to make it to the library roof from the sidewalk roof," Damon says. "It's a stand-alone building. We'll have to drop down and go in from the ground."

"And how the hell you plan on climbin' down from the auditorium?" Chad asks.

Jaime waves him off. "We can use extension cords," he says. "We got tons of them in the patch room. They'll hold."

"So how about gettin' off campus, then?" Chad asks.

"Much as I want out of this place, I don't think we focus on that. Not yet," I say. "The priority is Mackenzie. This is a . . . dress rehearsal. We get her, we come back here, then we talk about the car. I mean, Jaime's right, this is probably the safest place on campus."

"What about Laura and Cammy?" Chad says.

I start to respond, but Jaime cuts me off. "Bri, unless you know where she is, we can't plan for that yet," Jaime says. "You know we can't. Not successfully."

Shit.

"Fine, but we'll still have to make it back here," I say. "And all the doors are boarded up. You plan on climbing back up to the roof from the sidewalk while those things are coming after us?"

"Helicopters," Kat says.

"Yeah, um, we don't have one of those," Travis says.

"No, I mean, we saw some in the air," Kat goes. "Downtown. We could paint something on the auditorium roof in case one flies by. We got plenty of paint."

We all nod. It's a good idea. And thinking of what we saw from the roof gives me another idea.

"What about a distraction?" I say. "We could take a bunch of stuff up to the roof and start chucking it down at the parking lot. I don't think it'd scare them, exactly. I mean, they're pretty fearless. But it might keep them busy in the lot while we're working our way north over the sidewalk."

"What kind of stuff?" Jaime asks me.

"Anything," I say. "Props, lumber, lighting instruments . . ."

"Whoa," Jaime says. "Those lights are two, three hundred bucks apiece."

I let my expression go neutral and simply look into Jaime's eyes. It only takes about three seconds for him to grimace and say, "Right. Sorry. Okay, we'll have Dave handle the paint and the diversion."

"So how do we get back in?" Damon asks.

"Headsets," Jaime says. "We have wireless headsets for the plays. For the stage manager and the tech booth, like when a show is running. We could use those. Put Kat in charge of one, and signal when we're on the way back. They could unboard the hall doors and let us in."

"Hey, wait a sec," Kat says. "I'm coming with."

"No, you're not," Jaime says. "You stay behind and get some people ready to take those boards down when we say." Jaime swallows hard. "And if something happens to us, they'll listen to you," he adds quietly.

I ignore his implication. "That also means leaving these behind," I say, lifting one of the screwguns off our weapons table. In order to make it quick, they'll need both DeWalts to take down everything we've screwed into the doors.

"Yeah," Jaime admits. "Well, we got enough here to improvise."

We all nod at each other. Kat scowls, but goes to fetch the headsets anyway. There's not much she wouldn't do for Jaime. I wonder if they're secretly a couple or something. Because thinking about that for five seconds is better than anything else there is to think about right now.

Ten minutes later, we're back on the auditorium roof. Jaime, Travis, and I are armed with the Starfire swords. Chad grips a wooden baseball bat. Damon's got a length of steel pipe. We take a quick look around to get our bearings.

Our bearings indicate that we're in a whole heap of steamy shit.

The parking lot is a bigger dead zone than it was last time we were up here. Dozens of bodies are strewn across the blacktop. I scan the area desperately, looking for Laura's green hoodie, but the light is fading fast and the parking lot lights haven't snapped on. Still, I don't think she's down there. That's something.

We take count and agree there are at least forty infected students loping around, grunting, groaning, screaming, howling—

"Why ain't they attackin'?" Chad says as we look down from the edge of the roof.

"Looks like they did fine," Damon says, swallowing hard.

"Naw, I mean each other."

We fall silent and process this. Chad's got a point.

"They went after healthy people," I say. "Not other sick kids. So they're not just crazy."

"So . . . is this a good thing or a bad thing?" Chad asks.

The other four of us answer in unison: "Both."

We allow ourselves a terrified chuckle. Peeking over the edge of the roof, I see Keith still moping around the rolling door. The bone in his arm sticks out at an angle. I lurch back from the edge.

"The arms," I say to no one in particular. "They keep biting people in the arms and throat. How come?"

Jaime risks a glance over the edge. "In other words," he says, wrinkling his nose at the smell, "what's their motivation?"

"This ain't no drama class," Chad says.

"It's a basic truth," Jaime says. "Everyone wants something. Those people down there want something."

"They're not people," Chad says. "They're monsters. Zombies, like that kid said. What they want is to eat our fuckin' flesh and bones."

I start to correct my best friend, to remind him that he basically just called another of our best friends a monster—then blink as if there's something in my eyes. "Bones," I say.

"Yeah, bones."

I glance out at the parking lot. The infected students thump around down there, moaning.

I wonder if Laura is one of them. If that's why I don't see her body, because she's not dead, because somewhere on campus, dragging clubbed hands along the sidewalk—

Stop, I tell myself. *Just stop. Focus. Think.*

"They're infected, which means they're sick," I say slowly, trying to sound my way through my own thoughts. "There are two ways to fight an infection—either you shoot something into the body, like antibiotics or chemotherapy or something, or the body takes care of it itself, with the immune system."

"Sweet," Chad says. "So we skipped drama and went straight to biology."

"Bone marrow is part of the immune system," I say, ignoring Chad. "In a roundabout way. That's what was wrong with Kenzie. Her cancer attacked her blood and bone marrow. That's why they did a transplant after she went into remission. To try to keep the cancer from coming back. And *we* know these people have been going after bones. The arms, that one chick's leg. The neck, where the tonsils are. What if . . . what if they can sense that there are healthy people, uninfected people, in here, and something's making them seek us out?"

Travis rolls his eyes. "They can sense we're not sick because they can see us," he says. "It's pretty easy to tell us all apart. They're crazy, we're not."

"Not yet," Jaime adds quietly.

"But they're not *just* crazy," I argue. "If they were, they'd be tearing into each other too. They're specifically targeting us, not each other. They're . . . medicating."

"Uh, say that again?" Kat asks, squinting at me.

"Look, I don't know, but . . . the attacks we've seen. They don't attack each other, they only attack healthy people. Sucked on the . . . bones . . . maybe to get to the marrow."

"My grandma does that shit," Chad says. "It's gross."

"Your grandma eats people?" Travis says.

Miraculously, Chad chuckles a bit.

"No, look," I go on, trying to remember all the medical jargon I heard while Kenzie was sick. "The spleen, lymph nodes, tonsils. All part of the immune system. What if they can sense healthy immune systems, and they're going after the immunoglobulin?"

They stare at me.

"Who the hell are you, again?" Chad asks.

I grab my head with both hands, struggling not to deck someone. Maybe Chad.

"*Listen!* For some infections, people get injected with immunoglobulin, which is made from healthy blood," I explain. "It's like a boost to your immune system. Maybe that's what they're doing."

"Then send 'em to fuckin' Walgreens," Chad says.

The monsters below us bellow. We freeze for a moment.

"The disease won't let them," I say after a pause. "They're clearly insane; they're operating on a base instinct level. Those crystals, that stuff on their arms, that's got to hurt. Throw in an adrenaline dump, maybe . . . and they become what we've seen so far. Deformed people who can't feel any pain other than the pain of the sickness itself. No wonder it drives them crazy."

I wipe my mouth. For a moment, I'm sort of proud of myself. Which makes me think Mom would be too. And Kenzie . . .

"Okay, cool theory," Jaime says. "But regardless, we—"

He stops when a tan pickup truck careens along the deserted street beyond the parking lot. It must be going eighty miles an hour.

Damon runs to the south edge of the auditorium roof, waving his arms.

"*Hey!*" he shouts. "Up here! Over heeeeeere!"

No good. The truck has come and gone before the driver would have ever had a chance of seeing Damon.

Chad stares out at the street. "Lucky son of a—" he begins, but stops as a small red car follows the truck.

Next thing I know, Scarlet Avenue is a racetrack. Cars fly past one after another, right through the intersection at the southeast end of the school. They're all headed west on Scarlet. Fast.

I turn the direction they're headed and shield my eyes against the setting sun.

"Uh, guys . . . ," I say.

The guys turn to look in the same direction. I point. Like they could possibly miss it.

Three, maybe four miles west of PMHS is a freeway, the 51. From up here, we can make out maybe a mile's worth of its length. Traffic is backed up, bumper to bumper, not moving. Every few seconds a car jets out of line and attempts to take the shoulder, but it's stopped by another driver who already had the same idea. Three lanes of northbound traffic have become four lanes of parking lot.

And beyond the freeway, the fires have spread.

The largest is farther west than the 51, sending great plumes of black smoke into the crisp November air. I remember reading once that black smoke means the fire department hasn't contained the fire yet; only when it turns gray or white has it been doused.

"That's a lot of people," Damon whispers, still looking at the freeway. A moment later, we hear what can only be gunshots coming from that direction.

We instinctively duck, all of us but Chad. He only stands there, fists clenched.

"They're evacuatin'," he says. "That means it's gettin' worse. Musta been some kinda announcement."

"Maybe it's just rush hour traffic?" Travis suggests.

We all glance at him. Travis looks hopeful for just one second, then snorts. He knows the truth; we all do: even in rush hour, cars *move*. Some insane part of me wants to shout at the truck, the little red car, the others whipping past our school, "Turn around! Don't go that way! The freeway's clogged all to hell!"

The sound of tires screeching makes us all whirl east. A military truck of some kind, painted desert camouflage, barrels down Scarlet. Twice it smashes up onto the sidewalk to get past other vehicles. Probably headed for the freeway, for all I know.

"It's the Army!" Damon shouts, and races for the south edge of the roof. He waves his arms again at the cars rushing by on the street. "Hey!" he screams. "Up here! Help! Help us! Help uuuuuus!"

We join him at the edge and wait. It's too late for the military truck to have seen us—but a brown van slows down near the gate.

Seeing this, the rest of us start shouting with Damon. The wails of the diseased kids below croon with us, like we're dinner scraps on a table and they're dogs waiting for us to fall.

The van stops, earning honks from other cars behind it. I hate the other drivers with useless, white-hot intensity.

A white guy, his hair styled in an honest-to-god *mullet*, hops out of the driver's side and comes around to the front of the car. We scream ourselves hoarse.

That's when a flood of people on foot and on bicycles crosses the intersection of Scarlet and Twenty-Eighth, also headed west along Scarlet, straight for the dude with the mullet. They run full tilt, holding backpacks, duffel bags, suitcases, cardboard boxes.

"Oh, my god," Damon whispers, squinting through his specs. "That's Tara's dad."

"*What?*" Jaime says.

"The guy with the hockey hair, by the van," Damon says.

"I've met him. Tara called him before the line went down, right?"

"Maybe he saw the news and came after her," Chad says.

"Doesn't matter. He's got a van," I say. "Between that and the station wagon, maybe . . ."

The driver of the van—Tara's dad, and now that I know this, I can see even from this distance that he has the same shade hair color as hers—turns to see the flood of people coming at him, and hesitates.

Sick kids in the parking lot storm the fence and reach through the bars, trying to grab him, but he's too far away. Runners spot the sick students stampeding for the fence, and change course, dodging speeding cars to get to the opposite side of the street. One runner gets clipped by a blue pickup, sending him into the air and crashing to the street, where two other cars run him over. He doesn't move. The following cars merely swerve to avoid his body. No one stops.

"Look out!" Chad bellows.

We all jerk in every direction, assuming he's shouting at us. But he's not. He's pointing off to one side.

We follow the gesture and see another white guy, on foot, charging up to Tara's father, who looks like he's still trying to figure out how to get to us. The second guy shoves him to the pavement and kicks him in the face before running to the van door and getting in behind the wheel.

"*Son of a bitch!*" Chad screams at him. He turns and stomps the roof.

Tara's father gets to his hands and feet. By then his attacker has revved the van and driven into the fleeing traffic. No one tries to help Tara's dad up.

"Oh, no," Damon grunts. "Oh, god."

Tara's dad leaps to get out of the way of his own van. But the leap puts him too close to the school fence.

A dozen sick students reach through the white bars, and two get ahold of him. He gets jerked up and against the fence, hard. Somehow they manage to pull both arms, then both legs, through the spaces between the bars. The guy's head falls backward as he screams for help.

The group of sick kids tears into him, his clothes rapidly disintegrating beneath their hands and teeth seeking skin and bone.

We watch until we hear the first bone snap. Even from this distance, even over the shouts of the runners, even over the sounds of the cars rushing past . . . we hear it.

"Jesus," Damon says, his voice dry. "We're gonna die."

5:52 p.m.

"COME ON," I SAY. "NOW'S OUR CHANCE. MAYBE
with all the people running past, those guys'll be kept busy."

"Which guys?" Travis says, like he's trying not to puke.

"The monsters."

I lead the way to the north edge of the roof. My sister's down there, and not far away. Just have to get to the library and back. That's all. Just there and back. There and back. That's all.

And Laura—

I wish I hadn't broken up with her. Maybe it was the right thing to do, maybe it wasn't. I don't know. But if she's still alive . . .

No, I think. *Not now. Laura, I'm coming. I'll find you, I swear to god, but I can't go there now. Please be okay.*

Chad comes up beside me as Jaime and Travis tie one end of an extension cord to an air-conditioning unit, then toss the slack over the edge of the roof. Jaime's hands shake as he ties the knot.

"Hey, Bri," Chad says. His voice is quiet.

"Yeah."

"I got the keys to the wagon," he says. "After we get Kenzie, if we see a place to get outta here . . . a hole in the fence, or someplace those sickos aren't around . . . you wanna go for it?"

"Without Laura?"

"Hey, you know I got nothin' against her," Chad says. "Matter of fact, you're a fuckin' jackass for breaking up with her, you want my opinion. But I'm just sayin'. If there's a way off, do you wanna take it or not? Your call, man."

Temptation drives a cold steel spike into my belly. Get out of here? God, yes. Grab Kenzie, make a break for it, get to the familiar safety of the Draggin' Wagon, maybe make it back to Chad's, or to my house. Sacred ground.

Without Laura.

I see her vividly alive, crouching in some classroom, shaking wildly. Moaning softly, trying not to get sick with fear, or popping pill after pill after pill.

Leave her behind?

"No," I say. "Can't do it. I mean, I want—"

"Loud and clear, boss," Chad says. "It's off the table till we find her."

I punch his shoulder. Not very hard. Chad manages a pale grin and socks me back. Not very hard.

"Ready," Jaime says.

One by one, we scale down the makeshift rope. This puts us on the roof over the central sidewalk. The roof slopes down both ways, with a narrow I-beam in the center.

"Stay in the middle," Jaime whispers. "I don't trust this aluminum roofing."

We nod. The roof is made mostly of thin metal, designed only to block infrequent rain and more frequent sunlight. One heavy step onto it and you'd risk punching right through to the ground.

"Kat," Jaime says into his headset. "Come in."

I hear the headset crackle.

"We're over the sidewalk now," Jaime says. "Sit tight."

"Where is she?" Chad whispers.

"The orange doors," Jaime whispers back. "She and Dave got the screwguns ready for when we bolt back in." He looks at me. "Ready?"

I say nothing. I put my Starfire through one belt loop on my jeans, drop to my belly, and begin sliding my way along the I-beam. A second later, I hear the guys follow behind me.

I can also hear the wails of the infected, but so far, I haven't seen any since we looked straight down from the auditorium roof. The campus looks dead from this angle.

We're halfway to the library when we begin seeing the bodies.

I don't always see a full body, head to toe; mainly it's arms or legs sticking out akimbo on the sidewalk, not moving. Smears of blood dot the concrete. I look for Laura's forest-green hoodie, or the purple Vans she had on this morning. I helped her pick them out for her birthday a few months ago. She was in a good place that day, mentally speaking, as we walked around the mall and she tried stuff on. She's a basics kind of girl, one of the things I loved about her. She's not real big into makeup but still pulls off being a girl without being girlie, or going the other way and adding twelve *R*s to *grrrrrrrl* the way Kenzie kind of does—

A groan from the sidewalk surprises me and almost makes me scream. Damn it, I have got to get my head in the game or it's going to get me killed.

I stop, raising myself up on my elbows, and scan the area quickly. I see right away where the sound came from.

The guys behind me stop too. We all gape at the sight.

Twenty yards ahead on our left, the cafeteria doors hang from broken hinges. Nearby, one of the infected kids, a football player, crouches over a teacher. The teacher isn't moving. The football player holds one of the teacher's forearms in both disfigured hands, his teeth tearing into the flesh like it's a chicken drumstick. Wet, slurping sounds spill from the kid's mouth as he spits out the muscle to get to the bone. I get the distinct impression that the sick kid is making do with a corpse, that he'd really rather be chewing on living tissue.

I hear a strangled choke and look behind me. Damon's mouth is clamped shut, his ample stomach rolling. A second later, brown gunk spurts from between his lips. I turn away, feeling my own gorge rising.

I continue creeping slowly along the beam, trying like hell not to let the football player hear me. We're safe enough up here; there's no way for him to reach us even if he does spot us. But I'm also pretty sure if he sees us he'll follow us along the sidewalk, waiting for one of us to jump down. Or fall.

I also figure—or rather, hope—that between the five of us, we could take him down if we had to. But the noise might attract others, and then we'd be overwhelmed.

And besides . . . I mean, he's just some *kid.* Up until a few hours ago, he wouldn't have even registered on our radar—he's a jock, we're not, move along. Now, though . . . now he's just some kid who was probably getting all jazzed up about the game tonight, right up until the infection hit. It's almost ironic; me and the guys tended to think of the athletes as sort of inhuman or untouchable, as being above the rest of the world. Or thought that *they* thought they were, anyway. Now he's sick, *beyond* sick, and probably killed that teacher and who knows how many others. What will we do if we do have to fight? Sure, he's a threat, and we have every right to defend ourselves, but he's still just like us. Just a student. Just human. More like us than I ever thought.

Only . . . dangerous. Bloodthirsty, in the most literal sense of the word.

So maybe not quite as much like us as I want to believe. Me and Chad and Hollis got in a fight last year with some top-shelf delta-bravo juice boxes in front of a movie theater. It didn't go too far; security came and broke it up before anyone needed stitches or anything. I knew even as I was trying to talk our way out of it that it wasn't going to work. Those assholes wanted a fight. Period. So I fought. Hated it. But did it. But I still had this compulsion to try not to, to believe that somehow reasoning would be enough.

It wasn't enough then, and watching that kid chew on the teacher's body, I realize it won't be enough now, either.

We keep crawling across the roof.

The jock doesn't notice us as we slide past the cafeteria. Farther ahead on the right is administration, but we can't see into it because its windows are underneath the roof. Just beyond that, the library. When we finally make it parallel to the library roof, I realize Damon was right; there's no way we can make it from here to the roof of the library. There are at least fifteen or twenty yards between us and the building.

When I look down at the front of the library, my heart seizes.

The windows have been shattered. Naked holes glare emptily at us. I can't see anyone inside, but then again, from our elevated angle, someone would have to be standing right at the windows for us to see them.

I look back at the guys. Jaime arches an eyebrow as if to say, *You still want to do this?*

I nod and stupidly check to make sure my Starfire is still in place. It occurs to me we could have looked for armor of some kind too; Chad at least has his leather jacket on, but the rest of us are just in T-shirts. We could've found something in the costume closet or shop to protect our arms, since that's where the zomb—where the infected students seemed to try to bite.

Jaime jerks his head. We slide around on our stomachs till we form a strange huddle of prone bodies.

"Chad should hold the rope," Jaime whispers. "The rest of us can shimmy down."

"Bullshit," Chad whispers back. "I'm going in."

"You're the biggest guy here," Jaime says. "If we got to climb back up, you're our best bet to anchor the rope."

Chad scowls at him but eventually nods.

"I thought we were going back to the orange doors," Damon says, still looking a bit pale.

"If we have to, yeah," Jaime says. "But if we can climb up here without attracting attention, we do that."

I'm personally not sure Kenzie can make the climb, but I figure we'll solve that when we come to it.

"I'll go first," Jaime says, not looking thrilled with the idea. "Then Bri, then Travis. If it's clear, Damon, you follow."

We all agree. Chad quietly takes a loop of electrical cord from Jaime and sits up, legs outstretched. Jaime's tied knots in it for handholds. Chad grabs one end of the cord with his left hand, loops the cord behind his back, and grabs the cord with his right hand as well. Then he loops the cord once around his right leg. He nods grimly.

Jaime slides his own Starfire through his belt, grips the cord with both hands, and tugs. Chad nods again. Jaime takes a deep, silent breath and slides over the edge of the roof.

The aluminum crackles noisily and we all tighten. We hear Jaime hit the concrete softly and watch him race to the library doors. He slides in through the main entrance, where we lose sight of him.

If there were any infected nearby enough to see him, chances are good they would have given chase, so Travis hurries to follow. I go next, and we run toward the library doors. I feel like a World War II Allied soldier crossing Omaha Beach, waiting for snipers to shoot my head off. Then I think of Kenzie.

Please, God, just let her be okay, please . . .

Travis and I make it to the library doors, panting. I start to tug on the handle, relieved we at least made it this far—

"*Look out!*" Chad screams from the roof.

Me and Travis spin, reaching for the swords tucked into our jeans.

Three zombies are careening toward us on all fours, mouths open, eyes hungry.

One of them is Hollis.

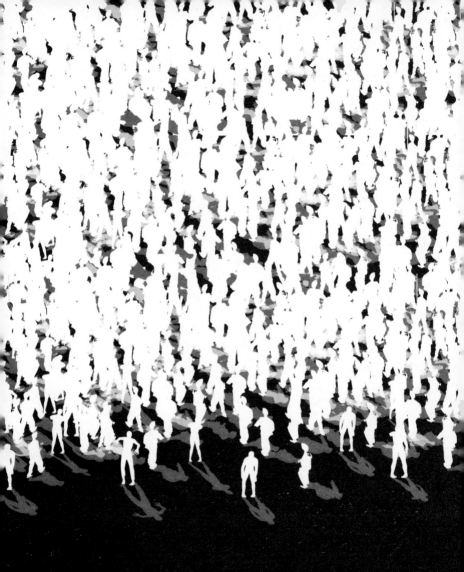

6:10 p.m.

"GO!" CHAD SHOUTS AT US.

I pull my gaze away from the monsters bearing down on us from the A buildings. As I move, I see Damon sliding down the sloped aluminum roof, and I imagine his fat ass carrying him right through the thin material; but the roof holds, and Damon is able to sail off and land on his feet—for a second. His legs crumple beneath him as soon as he hits, and I think, *Oh, god, his legs are broken, he's screwed* . . .

Damon's pipe clangs awfully against the concrete. The monsters see Damon hitting the sidewalk and collide with each other as they try to decide who to go after: us or Damon.

Damon looks up at me and Travis as we struggle to pull our swords out. Damon swallows once and meets my eyes.

"I'll get the gun!" he says.

"Damon, *no!*"

Damon climbs to his feet, spins, and bolts down the sidewalk toward the drama department and the parking lot behind it.

I don't move to stop him.

Hollis and another kid take the bait and sprint toward him like apes, galloping on their toes and knuckles, saliva dangling from their swollen lips. The third continues straight for me and Travis.

"Here we go," Travis says, his voice pinched, and lifts his sword.

Just as the infected kid passes under the roof, he's smashed flat by Chad. They both tumble against the sidewalk. Chad's baseball bat clatters away.

"Chad!" I shout.

The monster whips around and gets ahold of Chad's arm. He snaps his head down, trying to gnaw through the black leather.

Chad swears and gives the kid a combat boot to the ribs, breaking his hold. Chad skitters across the sidewalk, picks up the bat, and races back again, bat held high. The kid leaps, arms outstretched. It looks for one moment like his teeth have grown longer; then I realize it's that his gums have eroded.

Jesus, what *is* this shit?

Chad unleashes a roar and swings the bat. The end connects solidly with the kid's skull. There's a sickening, dull thump, and the kid drops flat. He picks himself up, shaking his head. Chad swings again. This time there's a crunch, and the monster lies still.

Breathing hard, Chad stands over his assailant. A patch of blood and hair clings to the bat. Chad studies this for a moment, looks back at the monster, then slowly backs toward us.

Travis pulls open the library door. "Come on," he says. "Before there are more."

We tumble inside. Travis yanks the door shut and slides his weapon through the handles as a makeshift lock. I start to point out that it's useless since the windows are busted, but keep my mouth shut. Maybe *feeling* safer is more important right now.

Chad slides to the floor, still holding his bat.

"I did it," he mutters. "I really did it, I really killed that kid, I really did . . ."

I want to say something to him, but all I can think about is Kenzie. I run to the librarian's counter, where they check out the books.

"Kenzie!" I whisper harshly. "Mackenzie, where are you?"

A stealthy creak escapes from behind the counter. The librarian's office door cracks open . . . and Kenzie pokes her head out.

"Brian?" she whispers.

Thank you, God, thank you thank you.

I vault over the desk, drop my sword, and hug her close as another girl looks out from the office door.

"I'm okay, I'm okay," Kenzie chants, and whether it's to me or herself, I don't know.

"What's going on?" the girl cries. I don't recognize her beyond being just another face in the high school crowd. She has longish blond hair, similar to Kenzie's.

"Shh!" Jaime orders. "Come on. Come with us, now!"

The girl obeys, skipping around from behind the counter. Her whole body is trembling, and I'm immediately reminded of Laura.

"Where's Laura?" I ask Kenzie, still smothering her against me. "Kenzie? Where is she?"

"I don't know," Kenzie says into my chest. "We were at the pep rally when this guy started attacking everyone and—"

"Brian," Jaime says. "No time. We gotta get out." He

thumbs the button on his headset. "Kat, we're on our way back. You ready?"

I take Kenzie's hand. "Come on."

"I saw her running toward the C buildings," Kenzie says.

Travis is at the doors, looking through the narrow inset windows. "Clear," he says.

I pick up my Starfire and lead Kenzie over to the doors. I look at Jaime, waiting for his order to go, fighting the urge to run full speed for the C buildings. If there's any chance Laura's there—

Jaime is standing still, staring into middle space. He hits the headset again.

"Kat?" He waits. "*Kat!*"

"Oh, for shit's sake. Really?" Travis grumbles. He pulls his sword from the door handles.

And is tackled from the back by a blur of purple blouse and gray pants that slams into him from behind a bookshelf near the door. No one even heard her coming.

The librarian.

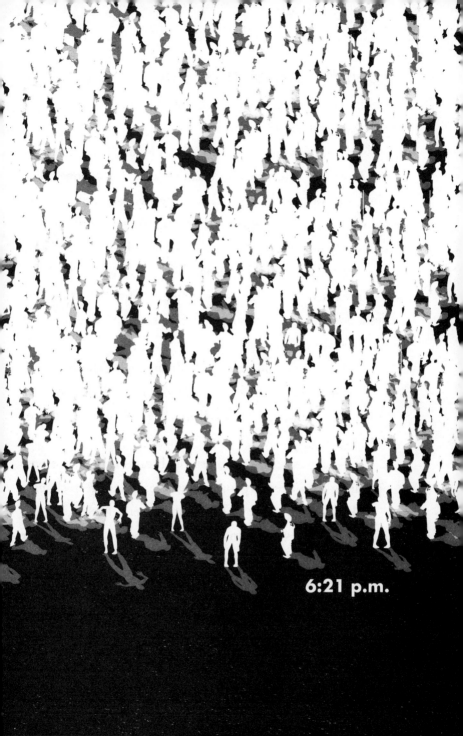

6:21 p.m.

TRAVIS'S SWORD FLIES OUT OF HIS HAND, landing with a clang several feet away. The nameless girl screams as Kenzie clutches me tight.

Chad leaps to his feet, bat in hand. There's a look in his eyes I've never seen before, not on Chad's face, not on anyone's. The librarian—once a nice older lady named Miss Hundley—is on top of Travis, a thing possessed, clawing and scratching at him, screeching horrifically. Her wicked, clawed hands rake Travis's face, tearing flesh from his cheek.

Travis screams, arms pinwheeling against her crystalline flesh. Something brittle snaps off of Miss Hundley. A piece of her arm. She doesn't care.

Chad stalks behind her, takes aim, and swings for her head.

The bat catches Miss Hundley on one ear with a heavy thud that makes my stomach shrivel up. She falls limp on top of Travis.

Travis shoves her over and gets up, breathing hard, not even appearing to notice the gouge in his face. We all creep closer.

Miss Hundley's face looks like the others', like it's melted. Her jowls and lower lip hang inches below her jaw, exposing her bottom teeth. Her eyes are distended, projecting out from their sockets, yellowed. And she's dead, a mass of drooping flesh and crystalline limbs, her brain pulverized by Chad's weapon. Even in death, her back remains curled, shoulders hunched in some bizarre atrophy. For a second, I expect her to transform like a Hollywood werewolf, to regain her human form now that she's dead, but she doesn't. And I'm grateful.

"What—what is this?" Kenzie says softly, pulling away from me for a closer look at the librarian.

I grab her hand to stop her. "We don't know."

"Kat," Jaime says into his headset. "Kat, please come in. Kat!"

Silence.

"We might be out of range. *Mierda*," he spits.

A burst of static punctuates the stillness at last. Jaime closes his eyes with relief, listens, then turns to us.

"They're ready," he says. "We need to go."

"Follow me," Chad says. His expression is cold and stoic. He boots the doors open and stalks outside without waiting for anyone to respond.

The other girl, who looks to be younger than Kenzie, darts past us to fall in behind Chad. I follow next, holding Kenzie's right hand with my left. Travis picks up his sword, and he and Jaime close in behind.

Chad moves purposefully down the central sidewalk toward the drama department, both hands on his bat, ready to swing at anything that gets in his way. We swivel our heads in every direction, expecting an ambush. I try to ignore the corpses of students littering the sidewalk.

There's no sign of Damon at first . . . until we spot his glasses, the lenses crushed to dust beside a thick puddle of blood.

"*Mierda*," Jaime mutters again as we pass them. I can guess what the word means.

"We should look—" Travis starts.

"Too late," Chad grunts. "Keep going."

"Hey, man," Travis says. "We can't just leave him out here."

"We can and we are," Chad says. "Keep go—ah, *shit.*"

We all freeze as two diseased kids bolt onto the sidewalk from the cafeteria ahead of us, growling.

Hollis is one of them. He must not have wandered far from the library. His lips are wet with fresh blood.

Hollis and the second monster, the jock who was eating the teacher by the broken cafeteria doors, book toward us, snarling, saliva dripping from their mouths. The girl from the library cries out and breaks away from Chad. The jock tackles her to the ground and shreds her throat. Her hair splays flat on the ground like a fan, growing sticky crimson with her blood.

Then from my left, a red-and-white blur zooms toward the creature. Before I can even unstick my feet to make a run for it, this figure wallops the monster square in the middle of his forehead with a long stick of polished wood, knocking him backward. By that point, the blonde has stopped resisting and lies cold on the sidewalk. Her fingernails are painted red.

Hollis doesn't notice one of his own has been dropped. He gallops toward me. If there is anything human still in him, I don't see it in his eyes.

Then Chad's in front of me, bat held in both hands. As Hollis leaps, Chad charges forward, catching our friend in the chest and knocking him backward. Hollis recovers quickly and lurches for Chad's legs, bringing him to the concrete.

Hollis leaps on top of Chad, grunting inhuman sounds. He drops his mouth toward Chad's face. Chad throws up his hands to protect himself, and Hollis catches one in his teeth. He digs deep, chewing hard, shaking the hand like a dog with a fetching stick.

Chad growls right back at him, kneeing Hollis between the legs. Hollis doesn't seem to register what should have been a stunning blow. He just keeps gnawing.

Beyond them, the red-and-white blur I saw hit the other monster comes into focus.

Cammy.

She's raising a hockey stick like a samurai sword. She brings it down three, four, five times on the other monster's head until the jock stops moving. Still clad in her cheerleader outfit, where streaks of blood blend into the red-and-white pleats, Cammy looks over at Chad and her boyfriend struggling.

"Hollis!" she cries.

Hollis either can't hear her over the sounds he's making, or doesn't care. Groaning, I run up to him and kick him in the head.

It's hard enough that Hollis's hold on Chad breaks. It's all the time Chad needs to roll out from under him and scramble for his bat. He raises it high.

"It's Hollis!" I scream.

Chad hesitates. Hollis whirls. Chad brings the bat down with both hands. The rounded edge collides with Hollis's neck, and he falls flat.

Cammy screams again and runs toward us, hockey stick up. I think she's going to swing at Chad.

But Hollis's chest, malformed under his blue and blood-stained shirt, still rises and falls. He's out cold, but not dead. Not yet.

"Cammy, come on!" I yell at her.

"But Hollis—"

"Never mind, we gotta go!"

"Move, *now*," Jaime says, his face strained.

I start to follow Jaime to the drama department. Chad shakes his injured hand and swears, blood flying from the bite wound. Cammy races to catch up and joins our group without another word, looking over her shoulder at Hollis's unconscious body.

One of his arms twitches. He starts to roll over.

He's getting up.

Jaime calls to Kat over the headset. We reach the doors just as I hear one of the platforms hitting the ground in the hallway.

Jack's body lies curled up by the window. His throat is gone. Gaping, ragged holes pierce his forearms, and his eyes seem to have already begun to sink into his head.

"Is that Jack?" Cammy says as another platform slams to the ground inside.

I can only nod, not looking, staring at the door, waiting for it to open.

"What happened to Hollis?" she demands. "Why does he look like that? What's going on?"

No one says anything.

The instant the doors crack open, Chad belts them wide and we tumble into the hallway. Kat and Dave hoist one of the platforms up and screw it back into the doors. With Jaime's help, they get the second one screwed in above it, sealing us in.

Jaime takes Travis by the shirtsleeve and guides him toward the drama hallway as Travis touches and touches again the wound on his face.

"There's a first aid kit in Golab's office," Jaime says. "Chad, come on, man. We got to get you wrapped up."

Chad doesn't follow. Kenzie and I slide to the tile floor. Dave and Kat look like they want to ask questions, probably about Damon, but they think better of it and move away from the doors. Cammy leans against the wall.

Kenzie nestles her face into my shoulder. "I'm sorry," she whispers.

"What about Laura?" I say as I try to catch my breath. "What did you say about the C buildings? Is she there?"

"I don't know. I think so," Kenzie says, dragging the backs of her hands across her wet cheeks. Tears have streaked down her face, smearing her trademark eyeliner, but she's not sobbing at all. "She ran that way, to the right. We were all running out of the gym and it was—"

"To the right?" I say. "So, wait, the west side, the west set of the C buildings?"

"I don't . . . Yeah. Yeah, the west ones. Brian, god, I'm so sorry. We should have looked for her."

"It's okay," I mumble over her head. "It's okay, we'll go back. We'll go back."

When I meet Chad's eyes, though, I wonder if it's true. His gaze drops to the bloodstained bat, which he drops. He watches it roll awkwardly across the floor.

"Fuckin' zombies," he says.

"Yeah," I say.

My voice shakes. I hug my sister close and don't fight the tears that start dripping down my face.

"What about Hollis?" Cammy demands, leaning on her hockey stick. Must've gotten it from the gym. "He said he was sick last night, and then during the rally . . ."

Chad and I both look at her. Cammy swings her head from one of us to the other, then looks at the floor.

Outside, I hear inhuman howling. Craving.

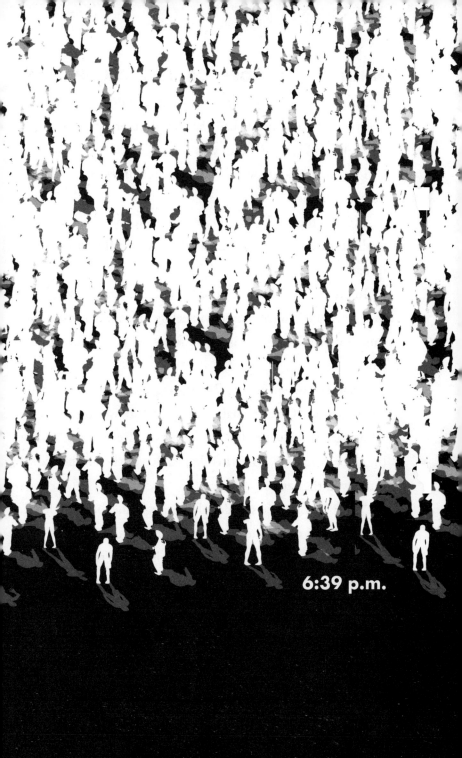
6:39 p.m.

WHEN WE'VE MORE OR LESS CAUGHT OUR
breath, I take Chad, Cammy, and Kenzie into Golab's office.
Everyone huddled in the hall watches our every step.

"Where's Damon?" John says.

I shake my head. Amid the random sniffles and moans, I hear Serena gasp.

I ignore them. Kat and Dave start to follow us, then seem to think twice about it, and sink down to the floor in the hall instead.

In the office, I shut the door behind me. Travis is seated on the grimy vinyl couch. Jaime is kneeling in front of him, taping gauze to Travis's face. Travis takes the procedure stoically, gazing emptily at a wall.

Chad sits down next to Travis, resting his bat beside him. Cammy takes Golab's chair and spins listlessly on it, never releasing her hold on the hockey stick. Kenzie sits against the door, knees up, forearms draped across them. She scowls intently at the carpet.

"So," Cammy says suddenly through the brittle silence, "anyone want to tell me what's going on out there?"

No one replies. Finished with Travis, Jaime takes a look at Chad's hand. Lips pressed together, Jaime dumps a quarter bottle of hydrogen peroxide over the wound.

"Holy mother!" Chad shouts, jerking his entire body. But he keeps his hand still.

"Sorry," Jaime mutters. He rifles through the sparse contents of the first aid kit. He meets my eyes for one brief instant.

The look on his face says it all. Things just got a lot more complicated.

I rub my face as Jaime winds gauze around Chad's wound. When he's done, Chad flexes the hand into a fist several times.

"Nice job," he says. "You a nurse?"

It's supposed to be a joke. No one laughs. No one smiles.

"Chad . . . ," I start to say.

"Uh, hello?" Cammy says, waving a hand. "Head cheerleader talking. What is happening, huh? Anyone?"

The last thing I want to do right now is recount the day's events to our friend. But behind her bluster, it's obvious Cammy's just as scared as the rest of us. And since she's armed and bloody and has already seen her boyfriend attacking Chad, the least I can do is bring her up to speed.

So I tell her the entire story, starting from the time we got to Chad's this morning, which seems like years ago. Cammy is silent, taking it all in.

"So now anyone who got bit by someone who has this disease or whatever—they become like them?" she asks when I'm done.

Cold quiet settles over the room as, one by one, we turn to look at Chad.

If Chad's upset by this, he doesn't show it. "Looks that way," he says carelessly.

"We're going to have to talk about this," Jaime says carefully. He's positioned himself away from Chad, on the other end of the small room.

"I feel fine," Chad says. "And what about good old Trav there?"

Travis touches the bandage. He, strangely, has not moved from his seat beside Chad on the couch. "It was her hand," he says. "And I don't think any of her spit or blood got into it."

"It's only been, like, ten minutes," Jaime says. "Who knows how long it takes to take effect?"

"Hold up," I say. "Cammy, you got a phone on you?"

She lifts one pleat of her skirt. "Which I would keep where?"

"Damn it."

"Yeah, tell me about it. One second we're out on the floor doing a routine, and the next . . ."

Cammy lifts her shoulders as if for protection.

"Craziness," she says. "Some dude comes tearing into the gym like a mad dog. Then a few more. Turned into this big throwdown, and I saw some of the toughest guys in our neighborhood get smacked down flat." She shakes her head. "Seen a lot of rough stuff at home, but nothing like that."

"Are there any other . . . you know," Travis says.

"Survivors?"

"Yeah."

"Probably. I hid out under the bleachers for a little while, and the stuff I saw those kids doing . . . eating . . ." Cammy shakes herself. "Anyway, yeah. A lot of people stayed in the gym after the lockdown call came through, but a lot left too. I think some made it over the fence by the tennis courts. Most of them just scattered. They're probably holed up in classrooms."

"How'd you get out?" I ask her.

"Through a window," Cammy says, shrugging. "Up high, at the top of the bleachers. Ran down the sidewalk. I hid out in a classroom for a while, over in A. Then made my way back to the fields, thought I could climb the fence out there. Found this." She pounds the stick against the floor. "And then two of those crazy-looking dudes came after me, so I took off. Hid in a lab. I was going to stay there, till I heard you all outside."

We take this in for a few moments. Then I turn to my sister.

"Kenz?" I say. "You still have your phone?"

Kenzie digs into her pocket and holds the phone toward me. I examine her face as I take the phone, looking for signs she's checked out or in shock, but Kenzie's eyes are bright and aware. That's good. It's *something*.

I wonder if Laura really made it to safety. Physically and otherwise. "You see Laura anywhere?" I ask Cammy.

"No," she says. "And why do you care all of a sudden? Thought you didn't like her craziness, or whatever you called it."

"I got over it." I open Kenzie's phone. "Let me try my mom," I tell everyone, and scroll through Kenzie's contact list until I hit Mom's number. I punch the send key, and then the speaker button.

The line rings several times. Just when I'm about to give up, Mom answers.

"Mackenzie!" she cries. "Honey, are you all right? Where are you? Where is your brother?"

"Mom," I croak, grateful to hear her voice. "It's me. Kenzie's here with me. She's safe."

"I'm okay, Mom," Kenzie calls.

I hear Mom sigh with relief. "Where are you?"

"We're in the drama teacher's office," I say. "You're on speaker. I'm here with the guys you talked to earlier. Chad, Travis, and Jaime. Cammy's here too."

"Hey, Mrs. Murphy," Cammy calls halfheartedly.

"Oh, thank god," Mom says. "I'm so glad you're all okay!"

"Mom, we sort of have a problem," I say.

"What? What is it? Are you all right?"

I clear my throat and avoid Chad's searing gaze. "It's Chad. Mom . . . he got bit."

Silence.

"What do we do?" I say.

"Chad?" Mom says. "Are you there?"

"Oorah," Chad says. "Alive and well."

"Chad, did the bite break the skin?"

"You could say that."

"How long ago did this happen?"

"Ten minutes, maybe."

"Where were you bitten?"

"Hand. Left hand. Just below the little finger."

"All right," Mom says, her voice becoming officious. "Clean and bind the wound. You have hydrogen peroxide? Some other antiseptic?"

"Yeah," I say. "We doused it pretty good."

"Good. Bind his hand, but not too tightly. No tourniquets. All right?"

"Okay . . ."

"Then immobilize the arm," Mom goes on. "As if it were broken. Wrap it to his body. Keep the bite below the heart."

Jaime immediately scours through Golab's belongings and finds a dark-colored scarf. He follows Mom's instructions, strapping Chad's arm down across his stomach.

"Do you have NSAIDs?" Mom asks.

"En-say . . . what?"

"Aspirin, ibuprofen, naproxen."

Jaime snorts a laugh and moves to Golab's desk. He opens a drawer and pulls out a huge bottle of ibuprofen and sets it on the desktop. "Plus Pepto, Tums, cough drops, you name it."

Yeah, I want to say to him, *because Tums are gonna be a big help here.* I take the ibuprofen bottle, gauging from the weight that it must be half full. Probably more than a hundred tabs.

"Um . . . yeah, we have those. Ibuprofen, I mean." I have to fight to keep the panic from rising in my voice. Mom's cool doctor's voice helps a little.

"Dose him with those," she says. "Give him twice what the label says, twice as often as it says to. Got it?"

I pass the pill bottle back to Jaime, who pours several pills into his hand, unlocks the fridge, and hands a small bottle of water to Chad. Chad takes it with a nod and swallows the pills. Jaime, god bless him, pulls out two other bottles of water, larger, and we begin passing them around. Then he stands in front of the open refrigerator like he's taking inventory. I can't see into it from my position. Funny, none of us thought to do that before we locked the fridge.

"Okay, what else?" I say to Mom.

"Chad? What kind of shape are you in? Overall. Pretty healthy?"

Even though she can't see it, I nod. Chad's always been a bull, but he really filled out after signing up for the Marines.

"I was gettin' in shape for boot camp this summer," Chad says. I notice Travis visibly react to that, like he can't believe it. "I'm prolly in the best shape I ever been in."

"Good. That might help. The disease spreads faster in people with preexisting conditions and those who aren't generally healthy."

"Like, on school lunch?" Jaime mutters, sneering at the carpet. "That's most of the class . . ."

"Brian," Mom goes on, "do you have access to any benzodiazepines?"

"Mom, I'm not a doctor. Speak English."

"I'm sorry, I'm sorry," Mom says. "Ah—Xanax? Serax? Valium? Tranxene? Libri—"

"Wait, wait, wait . . . Valium?"

"Yes."

My lungs constrict and sink into my stomach. My eyes shut. "How about Klonopin? Is that the same thing?"

"Sure, clonazepam or Klonopin would work. Brian? Do have access to any of these?"

I swallow something rancid. "Yes."

Travis and Jaime give me inquisitive glances. Chad, Cammy, and Kenzie do not.

"Very good," Mom says. "Get Chad started on them immediately. If it's a prescription that a student has, probably one pill every four hours. Chad, those will sedate you fairly well, if not put you to sleep. Increase the dose to once every two hours if the effects begin to wear off."

"What'll that do?" I ask, my throat dry.

Mom hesitates. "It will help reduce the likelihood of a violent outburst," she says carefully. "And Chad . . . I'm so sorry, hon, but if you were bitten by an infected person, you *will* become violent. That much is certain."

"How soon can you be here?" I ask. My legs have begun to shake.

"I'll get there as soon as possible," is her nonanswer. "I promise. The sheriff's office is doing a sweep through town here, door to door. We keep finding infected people. They're insane. They attack without any regard for their own safety."

Yeah, we know, I think to myself, and it's plain I'm not the only one thinking it.

"There's not much else I can do here," Mom goes on. "So I'm coming back to Phoenix. And I'm coming to get you."

"Mom, it's fucking anarchy out here. You can't just pick us up in Principal Winsor's office."

She doesn't correct my language. "I'm coming with two

sheriff's deputies," Mom says. "I'll be perfectly fine. You just stay put with your sister. We'll find a way in."

"Mom, please—"

"This isn't a debate, Brian. Stay locked indoors."

"But Laura's out there," I tell her. "In the school. Maybe alone. I can't leave her there."

Of course, now there's another reason I need to find her, but I don't bother explaining it to Mom.

"Brian, no. You don't do *anything*. You stay put."

"Mrs. Murphy?" Travis says. "Do you know anything more about this infection yet? What are we dealing with?" He's touching the wound on his face as he asks.

Mom sighs again. "The bacteria shares traits with Group A streptococcus, which leads to necrotizing fasciitis."

"I'm sorry, can we get that in American?" Cammy says.

"Flesh-eating disease," Mom says after a pause.

Cammy covers her eyes while everyone else looks at anything other than Chad. Chad sits motionless.

"That's not a medical definition," Mom adds quickly. "That's just something the media decided to call it years ago, rather sensationally. There's also evidence the disease causes a new form of gouty arthritis, the kind seen in some diabetics. That's what creates the crystal-like formations."

"So what's gonna happen to me?" Chad blurts.

"If what we've seen so far holds true," Mom says hesitantly, "your first symptom will likely be lower back pain, followed by pain in your joints as the gout spreads. Then tophi—the crystallized skin will start to appear, primarily on the chest, back, arms, and hands. Your eyes will likely jaundice, become yellow. And after that . . ."

Mom pauses again.

"G'head, Mrs. M," Chad says, only this time his voice cracks just a bit. "How long do I got?"

"It's hard to say, Chad," Mom says gently. "Some of the victims appear to have suffered the effects rapidly, while in others it's taken up to twelve hours or more. We just don't know."

"Define rapidly," Travis says, stroking the bandage on his face.

"Two hours to become symptomatic," Mom says. "That's a guess right now. The real danger is in determining when the patient loses control. That's part of the sinister nature of this contagion. If it was always fast spreading, we could catch it and stop it quickly. Unfortunately, we know now that symptomatic patients were treated and released over the last several days, only to become violent and unpredictable several hours later."

"Mrs. Murphy?" Jaime says. "I'm just wondering. The infection itself, is it fatal?"

"It doesn't appear so," Mom says. "But it's frankly too early to tell. It is horrifically painful, and maddening. Quite literally. It might be more merciful if it—"

Mom cuts herself off. I guess she remembers Chad's in the room.

Chad slowly leans back against the couch, staring up at the

ceiling. Just then, a bang sounds on Mom's end of the line. A blast. Like from a shotgun.

Mom shrieks in shock, which brings me to my feet. "Mom!"

"I'm fine, I'm fine," Mom says, breathing hard. "Oh, lord. Okay. Brian? You should be ready to isolate Chad in as safe a manner as possible until we can get him medical attention."

"What *kind* of attention?" I shout at the phone. "You said there was no cure!"

"Not yet," Mom says. "But we are working on it. Please believe me."

It isn't a matter of whether I believe her; of course I do. Something this big, this bad, hurting so many people—of course people are working on a cure. But how long will that take?

I guess it doesn't matter. I know what we have to do.

Over the speaker, we hear someone call out, "Dr. Murphy!"

"*Just a moment!*" Mom shouts. "Now listen to me. All of you. The best thing you can do is stay put. Communication with Phoenix has been sporadic. It might take some time, but I promise we will come and get you."

"What's the spread?" I ask. "I mean, how far has this thing gone already?"

Mom is quiet. It's enough of a response to make my skin chill.

"We're not sure," Mom says. "The government is having a hard time trying to pin down exactly how many cases there are. But they are definitely multiplying, and fast. The CDC and

Homeland are trying to come up with a public announcement, which will probably go live in the next hour, but it may be too late to do much good. And not everyone will see it. Panic has already begun, and now the priority will be coming up with a way to keep it reduced as much as possible."

I remember the rampage on Scarlet Avenue. The backup on the 51.

"At this point, people attempting to flee what they think is a bioterror attack are as much a danger as those with the disease," Mom says. "We've heard that local stations jumped the gun and advised people to get out of town."

I think about Tara's dad, who so heroically arrived in his van only to get carjacked and eventually . . . well, eaten.

"Mom," I say, "you've got to get us out of here. Use a helicopter or something."

"Brian, I'm trying," Mom says. "I am, sweetheart. You know I am. I'm terrified for you. But right now, stay locked indoors and stay as far away from these infected people as you possibly can." She pauses. "You're not the only ones," she adds softly.

We all stare at the phone. Mom seems somehow to guess what the expression on our faces is.

"There are other schools," she says. "All grades, all ages. Day cares . . ."

Jaime, still standing in front of the open fridge, presses his lips together and clenches a fist. Thinking of his brother, I'm sure.

"Shopping centers," Mom goes on. "Libraries, office buildings . . . It's a big city, and police and rescue are stretched thin. The National Guard has been activated, *finally*, but you can't just say, 'Go help everyone,' and expect the wheels to move right away. It's a bureaucracy, with all the red tape that goes along with it. They don't know how to arm themselves, what the rules of engagement are, where to set up to launch an initial sweep. It's going to take time. They have to secure high-value areas first, like our nuclear power plants, the dams, that sort of thing. Otherwise the whole state could go off the grid."

"Can't you just mow 'em down?" Chad demands.

"Chad, no," Mom says firmly. "These are sick people. We wouldn't 'mow down' people with AIDS or bird flu or plague. Brian, Mackenzie?"

"Yeah," we say in unison.

"I love you," Mom says. "Stay quiet, and stay locked indoors. The bacteria affects the brain, and the infected are extremely dangerous."

Chad grins helplessly and shakes his head in disbelief, as if to say, *Yeah, tell me somethin' I don't know.*

Then from Mom's end of the call, I hear someone shouting, "Move, move! Coming up the alley!"

"Oh, my god!" my mother screams. "Behind the van, behind the van!"

"Mom!"

"Miguel, this way!" Mom shouts. "This way, behind the—"

Some guy yells my mom's name. "Get back!"

The line goes dead.

I put the phone to my ear for what feels like ten years. Finally, I close it.

"What happened?" Kenzie whispers.

I stare at the carpet. It's old, threadbare, puke colored.

"Brian?" Kenzie's voice floats toward me through a tunnel, bouncing in the empty space between my ears. "What was that?"

"Doesn't matter," I say, my voice hollow. "We're on our own." I hand Kenzie her phone back. "Be careful with that," I say quietly. "It's our only line outside right now."

Kenzie nods seriously and puts the phone back into her pocket. Her scowl hasn't budged. No one looks at us.

In the silence, Travis says quietly to Chad, "You joined the Marines?"

"Yeah, so?" Chad says. "What, you hot for guys in uniform or somethin'?"

"My dad was in the Army," Travis says. "So was his brother. My uncle Steve." He takes a sip from his water bottle. "He hates me too."

Chad says nothing.

"Of course, it doesn't help that I'm a *fag*," Travis says, trying to laugh. "Least that's what Dad says." He takes another drink.

Chad remains silent, eyes flicking from one spot on the carpet to another.

No time for a big cuddle-fest. I give myself a mental slap,

telling myself that Mom is surrounded by police. She has to be okay. Has to be.

"So the clock's ticking," I say to everyone, hunkering down and pinching the bridge of my nose, trying to come up with an alternative to what I know has to be done now. "We should ask the kids in the hallway if they have any of those medications."

"If they do, it'll be in their bags," Jaime says. "In the Black Box."

"Still got to ask. What are you looking at in there?"

Jaime blinks, as if just realizing he's still holding the refrigerator door open. "Today's Tuesday."

"Uh, yeah?"

"Golab cleans out the fridge every Friday," Jaime says. "In terms of food, we're looking at a can of Diet Coke, one more bottle of water, and something that I can only hope is some kind of goat cheese." He tries the freezer. "And exactly one frozen personal pan pizza. Also, ice."

He lets the doors shut, then abruptly shouts something in Spanish. I don't need to speak the language to know what he's saying.

"So that means—" Travis says, then shuts up.

"It means we'd better ask about those meds," I say, avoiding Chad's eyes.

Jaime goes to the door and cracks it open after Kenzie scoots out of his way. He calls to Kat and quickly describes what we're looking for. Kat heads for the stagecraft students and Jaime closes the door again.

"Okay," I say. "We've got two hours. Maybe more, but let's say two. Plan A, ask the drama kids. Hopefully, someone in the hall has Valium or something like it."

"If not?" Travis says.

"Then we have to gear up for Plan B." I turn to Chad. "Dude?"

"Yeah, Bri."

"What do you want to do, man?"

Chad gets to his feet. Picks up his bat in his good right hand. We all tense visibly.

"Think," he says. "Just think. I'll be by the doors. I know where you're headed with this. I'd better rest up."

With that, he walks to the office door, opens it, and steps through, headed toward the double orange doors.

I slowly close the office door behind him.

"What's he mean by that?" Travis says.

I make eye contact with Kenzie. She nods, and swallows hard.

"Let's get some rest," I say. "Just—a little bit. Half hour."

Travis looks incredulous. "Hey, you heard your own mother," he says. "We got to figure out what to do about Prince Charming out there. Like, now."

"Half hour," I repeat. "I got a plan, but I need to think about it. Okay?"

Jaime takes a deep breath, then picks up his red duffel bag. "I think he's got the right idea," Jaime says. "I'm going up to the roof. Think."

"Mohawk out there might have, like, an hour before he goes ballistic," Travis warns.

"Yeah, and you might too, for all we know," I say. "Let's give him the benefit of the doubt, all right? Thirty minutes."

Jaime slides his Starfire through his belt and heads for the door. "We'll meet back here."

"Sure thing," Travis says with disgust. He crosses to the door and gives me a direct gaze. "I hope you know what you're doing."

"Don't push me right now, man."

Travis, about three-plus inches taller than me, considers for a moment, then nods.

"Cool," he says. "I'll push you in thirty."

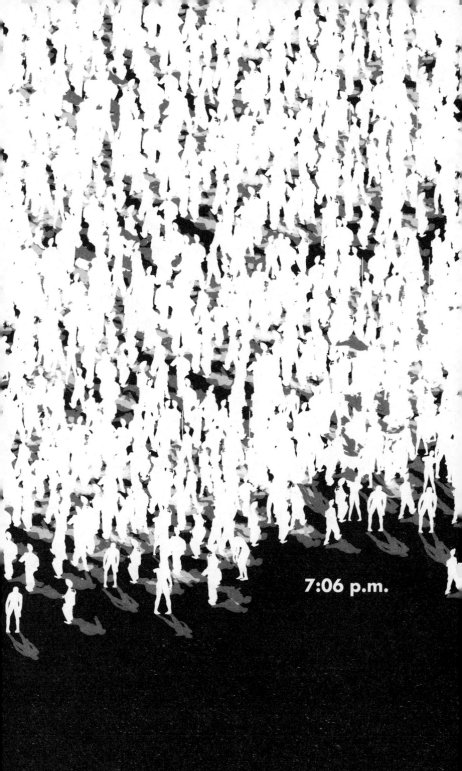

7:06 p.m.

"I'LL SIT WITH CHAD," CAMMY SAYS, STANDING
up as the door closes behind Jaime and Travis.

"You sure?" I ask.

"I'm fine, Brian," she says. "Now we know what we're dealing with, what to look for . . . I'll keep an eye on him."

"Thanks, Cammy."

"You got it." She walks out, hockey stick in hand.

I look at Kenzie, who's now standing against one wall, her arms wrapped around her middle.

"Hey," I say to her. "You want to lie down or something?"

Kenzie shakes her head. "I need to move," she says. "We were crouched in the library for so long . . . standing is good right now."

"Okay. How you doing?"

Kenzie lifts her chin, and the smile she pulls on is grim. Determined.

"I don't have cancer, if that's what you mean."

I can't stop a pathetic chuckle from escaping my throat. I pull her to me again and hug her tight.

"You're shaking," she says.

"Maybe *you* are."

"Maybe I am." She pulls back. "I didn't go through a year of hell to get eaten up by some freshman," she says. "We're going to make it."

At that moment, I crash headlong into a disconcerting truth: until my sister said it, I didn't really believe it. I talked big and I thought big, but the reality is, until just now,

I did not believe any of us were going to get out of here alive.

Kenzie's gaze is sharp, glinting. There are also circles under her eyes, and I imagine mine don't look much different. But you don't go through something like she did without getting something out of it. In her case, I think it's fearlessness. Strength.

Will.

"I might need to borrow some of that," I say.

"Some of what?"

"Nothing. Forget it. I need to go talk to Jaime. You staying in here?"

"Actually, I think I'm going to pee, if you must know."

That same tired chuckle drops from my mouth. Except *tired* isn't a big enough word for what I'm feeling. It's like every ounce of energy has been squeezed out of me from the top down until I'm nothing more than a husk.

We walk out of the office. Kenzie heads for the restroom as Kat comes up to me. Her eyes are red and squinting.

"Some of them have been asking about food," Kat says, glancing back at the students lining the hallway. "What do you want to do?"

"I'll ask Jaime," I say.

"Jaime's on the roof. He didn't want anyone to bother him. I left him alone." She looks disappointed.

"How's Travis?"

"Okay, I think. He's, uh . . . in the bathroom. With Dave."

It takes me a second to process what she means. "Wait . . . *Dave*? You mean, *with him* with him?"

Kat shrugs. "They've been flirting all year," she tells me. "I guess they figured, you know, time was short."

"Are they . . . like . . ."

Kat raises her hands. "Hey, I don't know and I don't need to know. But I'd knock before I go in."

I very nearly laugh.

"It's been quiet outside," Kat says. "Those . . . things are still out there, though. They bang on the doors sometimes. But Dave's moved the lighting instruments up to the roof, in case we need to throw them, like you said. And we're still surrounded. But . . ."

She trails off and bites her lip.

"But what?"

"It seems like there's more of them now," she says. "A lot more."

Oh, god.

"Okay," I say. "Thanks, Kat. I'm going to go talk to Jaime."

Kat nods. "Sure," she says. "And Brian?"

"Yeah."

"I asked around. No one has anything on them. Drugs, I mean. Sorry."

"Why am I not surprised," I say. "Thanks for trying."

Kat nods, and I head toward the auditorium. Some kids are asleep up and down the hallway. Serena, that senior chick, still cradles the blond freshman girl in her arms, rocking her gently.

I think the freshman has checked out, maybe for good. Even if we—

Even *when* we get out of here, she'll need some hard-core therapy.

She's not the only one.

In the auditorium, the lighting pipes have been lowered to waist height, and they're empty. Usually they're covered with heavy stage lights and hanging high overhead. The tall ladder's out too—the one we use to make focus adjustments when the lights are hanging.

I climb the spiral stairs to the grid, then make my way to the ladder to the roof. The hatch is open, and I see that it's dark out. The sky overhead is a strange orange color, and the air smells faintly of smoke. Before I even stick my head out of the hatch, though, I hear music.

Beautiful, soaring music.

I climb up. Jaime is seated cross-legged near the south edge of the roof, a violin beneath his chin. The tones issuing from the instrument are dark and deep. I don't make a secret of my approach, letting my feet crunch the little white rocks beneath my shoes. I notice, too, that someone has spray-painted HELP in enormous red letters that take up most of the roof. The paint is dry. Lined up along all four edges of the roof are heavy black lights. I've helped Jaime focus them over the stage before; they must weigh a good ten to twenty pounds each.

Jaime doesn't respond as I approach. I sit next to him. His

eyes are closed, face tight in concentration. I sit and listen, looking out over the city—or what remains of it.

There are too many smoke plumes to count, lit by the fires beneath them. On all sides, anywhere from a few blocks to several miles away, fires are raging. The sky is overcast with smoke, reflecting dim orange from the city lights beneath. I hear no sirens anymore. Scarlet Ave is empty except for the guy who was hit by the car, and what's left of Tara's dad, half stuck between the bars of the fence.

It hits me that we didn't tell Tara about him yet. Just as well. What good would it do?

"*Nero tocaba el violín mientras que Roma se quemaba,*" Jaime says, startling me.

"What's that mean?"

Jaime's eyes are still closed, face still knitted tight. "'Nero played the fiddle while Rome burned.' Seemed appropriate."

"Dude. Jaime. I had no idea. I mean, that you could play like that."

Jaime draws the bow across the strings, holding a low note, then stops. He opens his eyes.

"Yeah, well. Not a lot of Mes'kins around here working the violin, you know. Need to keep a low profile. Don't want to get jumped."

I chuckle, but only a little. Then I stall, because while I need to have a conversation with him, I'm also afraid of how he'll respond. "What was that? That you were playing."

"Beethoven. Violin Concerto in D, second movement. You like it?"

"Yeah. You're real good."

"Thanks." Jaime takes a deep breath and scans the horizon. "They're not coming," he adds.

"What? Who?"

"Anyone. Cops, fire department. National Guard. No one's coming for us."

He says it was such certainty and hopelessness that I feel a chill. "Come on, man, my mom said—"

"This thing," Jaime says, spreading an arm to indicate the entire campus. "It's everywhere." He points with his bow. "Check them out."

I follow the point of his bow down toward the fence. It takes a second, but then I see them: three people, hunched and lurching, moving on all fours up and down Scarlet Avenue. Adults. One is in a police uniform. They discover the body in the middle of the road and race toward it. They sniff, poke, and move on. The dead are of no use to them, I guess. Not unless they're desperate, like the sick kid in front of the cafeteria.

"Oh, Jesus."

"Yep. Honestly, I don't think it's just in town, either. Not just in this state. I think it's the whole damn country. Maybe the whole world. We're going to die here."

"You don't know that."

Jaime snorts and shakes his head a little. "There's three ways for this to end, I figure," he says. "Been thinking about it quite a bit. One, we starve to death. Two, we go crazy and kill each other off, and whoever lives through *that* starves to death. Three . . . those zombie things eat us alive. That's it."

"So what do you want to do?" I say, kind of pissy. But I can't get up and leave, either. It's like I have to hear this before I tell him my plan.

Jaime shrugs. "I don't know. Nothing? Pray, maybe. Think about God, the universe, and my place in it. I don't know."

"So you want to give up? Kill yourself or something?"

"Crossed my mind."

I try not to let my shock show. I wasn't joking exactly, but it's not like I *meant* it.

"But no," Jaime goes on. "I thought a lot about that, sitting up here. Thought about all the different ways I could do it. But I can't go through with it. I might wish I could've if one of those zombies gets ahold of me. But right now . . . no."

"So you haven't given up *all* hope." I can feel myself getting fidgety. I've got to talk to him about my plan, but if I push now, I'm afraid I'll lose him. My stalling has backfired. Now I'm just wasting time.

"Not yet. I think it's in the mail, though. You thought about it?"

"What, killing myself? No."

"Eh," Jaime says. "Dying in general. As in tonight, let's say."

"No," I say. "Not really. I think I'm going to make it. I think we're all going to make it." I don't tell him that I didn't reach this conclusion until a few minutes ago.

"Those of us who made it this far, you mean."

"Well, yeah. I guess. There must be some reason we survived this long."

Jaime grunts. "You believe in God?"

"Right now I think it's probably more important that he believes in me."

"That's pretty deep, *amigo*."

"Yeah, well. I'm not giving up. That's all I know for sure."

"How come?" Jaime's voice is remarkably probing.

I arch an eyebrow. "How come I'm not giving up?"

"Yeah," Jaime says. "I mean, is it just self-preservation at this point? Base instinct? Their will to eat us alive versus our will to survive? What?"

I'd never thought about it. Hell, when would I have? I start to tell him it's instinct, but then my gaze goes back to Tara's dad, dangling from those goddam wrought iron bars . . . basically having given up his life to try to get her out of this.

"Your dad live with you?" I say. I'm disgusted by the sight of the man caught in the fence, and disgusted that I no longer need to turn away.

Jaime doesn't answer immediately. And when he does, it's a simple "No."

"Me neither. Chad too."

"And Kat. Jesus. Talk about an epidemic, hey?"

For one weird, surreal moment, it's actually peaceful up here, watching the apocalypse unfold below us in our high school parking lot. The particular orange shade of the sky would be pretty under different circumstances.

Maybe I really am losing it.

"So, yeah," I say, mostly to startle myself back to reality.

"Fuck anyone who wants to give up. Not me. Not ever, not on anyone. We have to be better than them."

"Better than—" Jaime begins. Then he stops, grins a bit, and says, "Ah. Roger that."

He puts his violin back in its case without closing the lid and looks out over the city.

"You seen that show on TV?" he says. "The one about what happens to the planet after people are gone?"

"Sounds familiar, yeah."

"If it's as bad as I think it is, we're only going to have power for another day or two. A week tops, unless someone's able to get back in control. So what do we do then? How do we handle the crowd in the hall when the lights go out, you know? And without food, where does that leave us? How much time do we have before we melt down?"

Something greasy unrolls in my gut as I process where he's headed.

"I mean, look at us," he goes on. "We're a petri dish of social study here. We're like lord of the goddam flies. How soon before we turn on each other? Go, like, feral or whatever? Start raping the girls, killing each other off, just going batshit crazy. When the food's gone, the power's out, these things stalking around . . ."

I swallow hard. I taste air tinged with the odor of smoke and rotting flesh from the school below.

"I've been doing some math," Jaime says. "If there *are* other survivors here at school, they're probably in classrooms, and they're expecting the police to come get them. Soon. They can't possibly have much food, or any water. Eventually, they're going to leave. One by one, or all at once, they're going to leave. There's probably three dozen conversations just like ours happening all over campus. And you and I both know they're not going to make it. No one else has a view like we do from up here. They might see a couple of zombies roaming around and think they can outrun them, but they don't know how many there really are. We can assume their phones aren't helping them any more than ours helped us. They're going to run for it, Brian. And when they do, most of them won't make it. Then *they'll* turn into more zombies. See what I'm saying? Sooner or later, this whole campus, or a damn fine portion of it, is going to turn bad."

He pauses, and snorts. "Or worse than usual, anyway."

"Yeah." I cough. "I get it."

"Now, you throw in our lack of food too. Trying to keep everyone calm and sane. It won't last."

"So, wait—now you want out too? For real?"

"Fucking A, I want out now too. I want to head over to Madison, see if I can find my brother. Take him home."

"Our houses might actually be more dangerous, you know. But my thinking is, at least at there we've got home-field advantage. Food, water. The most logical place for people who are looking for us to check."

"Agreed, *amigo*. So I'm on board. There's just one problem."

"Well, shit, that's a relief. Just one?"

Jaime smirks. "We have more than twenty people down there. They're not all going to fit into a station wagon. How do you plan on getting around that math?"

"Let's assume there's room for twelve," I say. "We've done that many before. Me, you, Chad. Travis, I assume, but we'll have to ask him. That's four. Cammy and Kenzie, that's six. If I—when we find Laura, that's seven. Room for five more. Who's it going to be?"

"Hold up. Laura? Man, I'm sure you love her or whatever, but we can't risk—"

"She's got that stuff my mom mentioned. Klonopin. She's got a pretty bad panic disorder. I've seen her on those meds. They'll work. On Chad."

"Oh, so all we have to do is find her, borrow her meds, and dose your buddy? Easy as that?"

"I didn't say it would be easy. But it's our best bet."

Jaime gets to his feet. "There's a good chance someone has pot," he says. "John, maybe. We could, you know. Smoke Chad out."

"Dude," I say, "Chad's straight edge."

"Serious?"

"Yes, I'm serious. What, you think because he's got a Mohawk he's all coked out or something?"

"You think because I'm in drama I date guys?"

"He's going into the Marines. He can't risk getting high." It then hits me what a stupid goddam thing that is to say. Smoking out is the absolute least of Chad's worries.

"Kat said no one had anything, anyway," I go on. "And . . . I got another idea. A way out of here, a way to get you to Madison."

"I'm listening."

"But not without Laura, and not without getting those meds for Chad," I say. "You won't make it as far as Madison without a car, and you know it."

Jaime considers this for a minute.

"All right," he says. "Shoot."

I glance at the open roof hatch. Time's running out.

"There's a good chance Laura's in the C buildings somewhere, the west side," I say. "We take a small group, like before. Me, you, Chad, Travis. Find Laura, dose Chad, then radio back to Kat. Kat and Dave, or whoever, they come out with a ladder—"

Jaime winces. "To do what with?"

"The tall one, the one you use when you're working on the lights? Tip it against the fence, like a ramp. Anyone could climb that. Just crawl up the ladder and hop down the other side. We beeline for Chad's car, and we're gone."

"You think someone like Serena's going to be able to climb over that fence?"

I blink. "Serena? No, no, she's staying here. The rest of them stay here."

"Great. Do *you* want to explain that to everyone? 'Sorry, we're bugging out. You're on your own'?"

"I think we just ask. Throw it open. See who wants to give

it a shot. Thing is, one way or another, anyone who wants out will have to get over that fence at some point, probably while being chased down by those monsters. Honestly, I think most of them will want to stay put."

Jaime nods, as if considering this.

"So that's the plan," I say. "You still in? Or if you got a better idea . . ."

Jaime takes a deep breath. Out of nowhere, he soccer-kicks his violin over the edge of the roof. It crashes to the ground a second later in a quiet symphony of broken strings.

"All right," he says. "Time's a-wasting. Let's go get the troops."

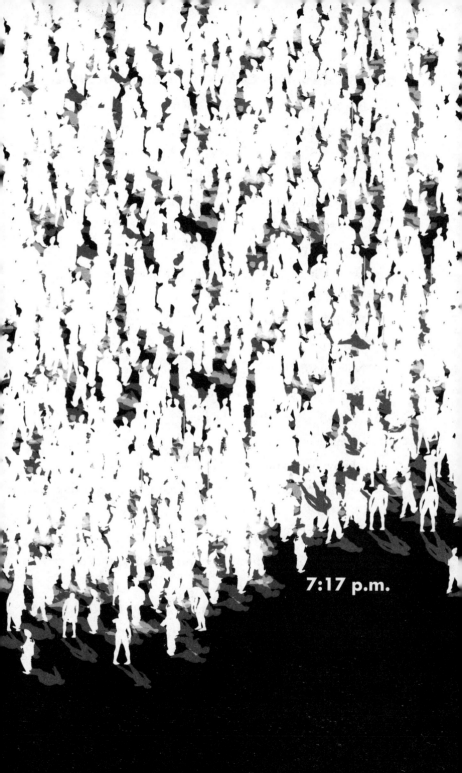

7:17 p.m.

I FIND CHAD AND CAMMY SEATED IN THE HALL BY
the boarded-up double doors, their backs against the wall.
Their weapons are within easy reach. They're playing Rock,
Paper, Scissors. I notice Chad's using his good hand. Cammy is
leaning over with her elbows on her knees, looking ridiculously
out of place in her bloody cheer outfit.

I almost laugh. Almost.

"Hey," I say.

"Hey," Chad says. Cammy tips her head back.

"You all right?"

"Peachy with a side of keen, Nilla Wafah."

"You sure?"

"Naw, man. I ain't sure of nothin' anymore. You?"

"Mostly the same. How's your hand?"

"Hurts like hell. But I'll be fine."

We make eye contact.

"I know what you're thinkin'," Chad says abruptly.

I sit down beside him, with Cammy on his other side.
"What's that?"

"That I'm gonna end up like Hollis."

I don't respond. Cammy stops playing the game and watches
us both.

"First sign of trouble, and I'm out," Chad says. "Okay? Take
those platforms down, and I'll head out. That's it."

"Actually, I had something else in mind. Come back to the
office with me."

Chad shakes his head. "Dude—"

Soft footsteps echo in the hall, and Kenzie appears from around the corner.

"Brian?"

"Yeah, sis." I get up and go over to her, moving some of her hair out of her face. That gesture reminds me of the girl from the library who got left behind. Who got worse than left behind. Red fingernails, long blond hair.

It could have been Kenzie.

It might be Laura.

I swallow hard and hug my sister close. She squeezes me back.

"I'm okay," she says suddenly. "Brian, I'm fine. I'm still here."

She said the same thing after waking up from the transplant. I hug her even closer.

"I know," I say. "Go back to the office, okay? We all need to talk about some stuff."

"Okay." Kenzie starts to go . . . then stops, walks over to Chad, and plants a gentle kiss on his cheek. "Thanks for coming after me," she says.

Chad doesn't move. "Yeah," he says.

"Meet us in there, like, soon," I tell Chad. "All right?"

"Sure, Bri. Whatever."

Then Chad calls my name just as I reach the turn in the hall.

I send Kenzie on to the office, then come back to my friend.

"What?" I ask.

Chad is still. Motionless.

"My back's startin' to hurt," he says in a monotone. "Just thought you should know."

My guts shrivel up.

Chad inhales deep through his nose. "I'll keep you posted. It ain't bad yet. You just take care of your sister. And if for one second you think I'm gonna hurt someone, you kick my ass straight out. Cool?"

"Uh . . . sure, man." I look down at Cammy. "How you holding up?"

"*Comme çi, comme ça,*" Cammy says.

"Is that French for 'Shut your ass, Brian'?"

Cammy grins. "Close enough."

"Listen," I say, "I'm . . . sorry. About Hollis."

Her grin evaporates. "Yeah," she says. "Me too. Sorry about Laura."

My body jolts. "Sorry? About what?"

Cammy blinks at me, like she's trying to backpedal. "Well . . . that she's still out there somewhere. That's all. I'm sure she's fine, Brian."

Adrenaline dumps into my stomach. Every nerve ending in my body lights up.

"Well, I'm getting her out of here," I say, and it comes out a lot more angry than I meant it. "All right? We're *all* getting out of here."

"Sure, okay," Cammy says, raising a palm. "It's cool."

Only it's not, and she knows it. I know it, Chad knows it

. . . every last damn one of us knows that we are far, far from being cool.

"We're getting out of here," I repeat.

"I know, I know," Cammy says.

"No," I say. "I mean now."

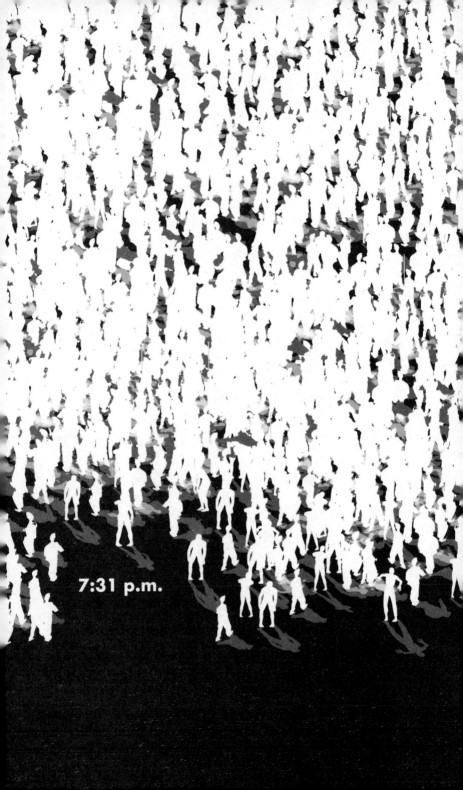

"YOU ARE OUT OF YOUR FREAKING MIND, BRIAN."

"You got a better idea? I'm listening."

"Yeah!" Travis says. He gets up from Golab's couch and points at Chad. "We kick this son of a bitch off the bus."

"Whoa!" Kenzie says, scowling at him.

"Yeah, I'd watch that mouth of yours, son," Cammy says, tightening her grip on her hockey stick. "That's one of my boys you're talking about."

This isn't going the way I hoped.

I spent the last ten minutes describing my idea, same as I described to Jaime on the roof. Kat's in the hallway now, spelling everything out to everyone else, explaining our options. Her job is to come back and report to us what the others want to do. I told our group everything about Laura, about her meds, and that—I thought I was pretty clear on this point—it's the best way to save Chad's life. With any luck. Even if it isn't a cure, it might buy us enough time for someone to *find* one.

I guess that isn't going to be enough for some people.

Travis folds his arms. "It's already been at least an hour," he says. "That leaves an hour if we're lucky before he starts turning into one of those things. Look, it's nothing personal, but Ten Ball here is a pretty big guy, and we can't risk him going blitzkrieg on us."

"He won't if we get to Laura," I say.

"You don't know where she is!" Travis yells. "You want to just wander the halls calling her name? No, that won't work, so

. . . huh. Okay, so we go door to door real quiet like? We don't have that kind of time."

"She's got to be in one of the west C buildings," I say, restraining my anger. "That's where Kenzie saw her last. She might have a hiding place over there, probably in a classroom."

"Chad?" Jaime says quietly. "How about you? How you feeling so far?"

"I don't feel no different," Chad says. "'Cept my back hurts." He holds up his good hand and tentatively curls it into a fist. "That hurts some too."

"Well . . . do you feel like killing someone?" Jaime goes.

"Just you, nutsack."

Cammy snorts. "Sounds healthy to me."

Jaime takes a hard look at Chad. "You're a dick," he states. "A white-trash bitch."

Chad, seated on Golab's desk, squints at him. "Are you, like, one of those *high-functioning* retards?" he asks. "Because I'll kick your Mexican ass square into next week, *ese.*"

Jaime leaps to his feet, tense. Chad squares up to him.

"You wanna go?" Jaime says, his lips pulling back from his teeth.

Chad throws a hand into Jaime's chest, sending Jaime back a few feet. "Fuckin' let's do this, then!"

"Hey!" Kenzie shouts.

"Those are my people I have to take care of!" Jaime shouts, pointed toward the hall. "And I'm not letting you wipe 'em out!"

"'Your people'? What're we, on the rez now?"

"Guys—" Cammy says.

"I'm not letting anyone else get hurt," Jaime says. "And if that means I got to throw your ass out of this building, then I'll damn well do it."

"Ah, boo-hoo, ya fuckin' pussy."

"*Shut up!*" I shout.

This pauses them for just a second, long enough for me to move between them.

"We cannot do this now," I say, swiveling my head to glare at them. "Too much shit's gone wrong already. We need our heads in the game. Got it? We've got a plan, and we have got to work together on it."

"Last plan got Damon a little bit dead," Travis says.

"*And* it saved my sister."

Travis hesitates, then shrug-nods an agreement.

Jaime stares hard again at Chad, then he relaxes too.

"All right," Jaime says. "I was just checking."

"Say *what*?" Cammy asks.

"Needed to see if our good buddy here still had some self-control," Jaime says. "And it looks like he does, for the moment. Sorry, Chad. I didn't think just asking you was going to answer the question."

Chad looks like he doesn't know what to do with that. He sniffs and shrugs. "S'cool," he mutters.

Man, was *that* a big goddam gamble. Still—he's proved the point.

"We probably have more than two hours from the time he got bit," I say. "He's in good shape—healthy, remember? But the clock's ticking. I know that. I've made my suggestion. And I'm going, whether anyone comes with me or not. But I really don't want to go by myself."

"I'm not going."

I turn to Cammy. She's not smiling, not frowning. But her jaw is set, her grip tight on the hockey stick.

"Cammy . . . what?"

"I said I'm not going," she says. "Someone needs to stay here with these freaks."

"Listen," I tell her. "You haven't been onto the roof yet, but the 51 is gridlocked. People are trying like hell to get out of town by the looks of it. And we don't know for sure if anyone's coming for us here or not."

"He's right, Cammy," Kenzie says. "You have to come with us."

"We don't know how long you might be here," I say. "There's only so much food."

"Brian," she goes, "why are you talking to me like I'm a fool?"

"Because I already lost Hollis and Jack today, and I don't know if Laura's still alive. I'm saving as many friends as I possibly can."

"Brian," she says again, "look at those punks in the hallway. If by some chance one of those things gets in here, you think these drama queers will be able to fight it off?"

"Don't call 'em that," Chad says. He's sitting down again, staring at the carpet.

Cammy cocks a hip. "What? 'Things'? That's what they are."

"'Drama queers,'" Chad says. "Don't call 'em that no more. 'Kay?"

Cammy arches an eyebrow and folds her arms. "*Chad?*" she asks. "Chad *Boris*? That you in there?"

Chad lifts his head. He has aged twenty years.

"It's been . . . a weird day," he says, glancing at Jaime and Travis. "And that shit don't help."

Cammy studies him for a moment. So does Travis.

Then Cammy nods. "All right," she says. "I take it back." She looks at me. "The point still stands. They're going to need some muscle, just in case. And if you beefy young gents aren't going to do it, then I will."

Jaime steps toward her. "Listen, sister, we're the only ones who—"

"*Sister?*" Cammy says. "Thought we weren't calling people names anymore."

"Okay, see, *this* is why we're going," I say, standing between them. "Because ten more minutes in here together will kill us all long before the monsters do. Jaime was right about that."

Cammy takes a deep breath. "I'm sorry," she says. "You all are going to look for help, right? If you make it off campus?"

"Of course."

"Fine, then. Do that. I'm staying here to play defense."

I think about the kids in the hallway. "Can you get them to listen to you if they need to?"

Strangely, Cammy smiles. It's weak, it's tired, but it's there. "I've been bossing around prissy white cheerleaders since August," she says. "This bunch has nothing on them. Trust me."

"We're not talking about making a human pyramid," Jaime says. "If you say run, they need to know where and how fast."

"Hey, relax. In a little while it won't be your problem, now, will it?"

Jaime tenses, and at that moment, I realize what it is he's worried about. This is his home away from home. In some ways, these are his kids. That's what he meant by saying "my people." Like he told me on the roof, he does want to get out of here; but he's afraid of what might happen to them without him.

"Jaime," I say quietly. "It's cool, man. Cammy can handle it. I swear. But if *you* decide to stay, we need to know that now, not out there." I think for a second, then add, "Out there it's not a dress rehearsal. Know what I mean?"

Jaime doesn't move, doesn't blink. Cammy stares him down. When Jaime takes another step toward her, she doesn't flinch.

"Take care of them," he says. "Don't let anything happen to them. Okay?"

Cammy flourishes her hockey stick and stamps the end down hard on the ground. For one moment, it looks like a medieval poleax.

"I'm on the job," she says. She resumes Golab's chair.

I scan the others. Mackenzie and Chad, Travis and Jaime. Kat opens the office door and slides inside, and I can't help but notice how quiet it is in the hallway behind her.

"They're staying," she says.

"All of them? You're sure?"

"Positive. They're too scared. They think someone'll be here soon."

"What about you?"

Kat glances at Jaime. "If Jaime's going with you, I want to stay here."

Jaime turns to her, surprised. "Katrina—"

"I don't want to see what happens," Kat says. "I've seen enough."

"I'm not leaving you here."

"Not your call, boss. I'm staying. Plus you guys need me and Dave to move the ladder. You make it that far, trust me, I'll be over that fence in a heartbeat."

"John could—"

"You really want to trust him on something like this?"

Jaime hesitates. "Okay. You and Cammy call the show."

Kat tries to smile for him but isn't quite successful. She leans up and kisses Jaime once, briefly, on the lips, then turns and goes back out into the hall.

"We ready to do this?" Chad says. He holds up his right hand for us to see. "I don't wanna piss on anyone's snow cone, but we better hurry up."

Around his knuckles, I can see swollen, crusty yellow sores. They glimmer under the fluorescent light overhead.

"Jesus," Jaime whispers.

I reach slowly for Chad's shirt. He doesn't stop me from pulling the collar down a couple of inches. Beneath the thin material, Chad's skin glitters. It's not bumpy, but more like scales.

I feel cold all over as dread climbs up my spine.

Jaime folds his arms and clears his throat. "Okay," he says. "So we hit the roof again like before, climb down to the C buildings. Find your girl. Book fast and hard for the fence. That about it?"

"Well, here's what I'm thinkin'," Chad says. His posture has gotten worse, his back starting to curl. It's not as bad as Hollis's was, but it's getting there. I wonder how long we've really got before he goes feral.

I wonder who else is wondering it. And what they're prepared to do about it.

I give myself a shake to clear my head. One thing at a time.

"They don't feel no pain," Chad goes on. "I gave my buddy Hollis a straight shot to the cash and prizes, and he didn't so much as blink. That leaves two choices. Cripple . . . or kill. As one of the soon-to-be freak shows out there, I'm votin' for the cripple. There might be a cure somewhere out there, and we gotta give those bastards a chance at it, *including* yours truly, if you don't mind."

We nod.

"Everyone got their gear?" he asks.

We all pat our various weapons. Kenzie's the only one without. Jaime offers to find something in the shop for her, but she only shakes her head.

"We give the key to the fridge to Kat?" I say. "I mean, in case we . . ."

"Right," Jaime says. "In case."

"Try the phone again," Cammy says. "Just to make sure."

Kenzie obediently takes her phone out. She checks the screen, then flips it open and punches in 911. Listens.

"Nothing," she says, closing the cell. "Sorry."

"Had to try," Cammy says, sighing. She stands and hefts her hockey stick.

Kenzie slides the phone into her pocket. "We're really going to leave everyone here?"

"They can't all fight, and we don't have enough weapons to go around anyway," I say. "If any of them change their minds about staying and want to try going over the fence on our way back from C, they know they've got the option."

"All right," Jaime says. "Let's move."

"One question," Chad says, standing in his way. He looks at Travis. "What's a ten ball?"

Travis blinks. "It's a pool ball. Like in billiards. It's white with a blue stripe."

He suddenly rubs a hand across Chad's Mohawk. And grins.

Chad tightens his jaw, and I think, *Oh, shit, we were so close too . . .*

Then Chad says: "Okay, fair enough."

I almost laugh. With that break in the tension, we go into the hallway together. May as well have entered a tomb; the silence is deep, penetrating, and unsettling, punctuated infrequently by a thump on the outside doors that echoes hollowly down the length of the hall. People are weeping softly, trying to hide it, but not trying too hard.

Serena is stalwart as ever. She still, even after all this time, is keeping an arm around that little freshman girl. Kat sits near Serena. Dave sits nearby, thumbing listlessly through one of Golab's acting textbooks. The girls he was holding earlier are curled up on each other a few feet away. I don't see John anywhere. And I don't care.

Dave gets up when he sees us coming out of the office. "I really want to come with you," he says, frowning. "But . . . I get it. You can count on me." He glances at Travis. "You all right, man?"

Travis conjures a smile. "Sure thing," he whispers.

"What happens if you don't come back?" Kat asks, looking right at Jaime.

"Someone will," Jaime promises.

I don't believe him. I don't think Kat does, either, but she doesn't argue.

Our team crosses to the auditorium doors as the freshman girl leans further into Serena, curling up, eyes closed tight, whimpering. Serena strokes her hair and says, "Shh, shh," over and over. Serena kisses the girl tenderly on the cheek.

One hand on the auditorium door, Chad turns to me and says, "Dude. That was hot, I'm not gonna lie."

I smirk back at him. Chad laughs tensely, then shoulders the door open. Kenzie and Jaime follow. I wait for Travis.

He and Dave are hugging each other tight. Travis's face is toward me, over Dave's shoulder, and he looks like he's fighting tears. Thing is, I can't tell if it's because he's scared, sad, happy, or what. Maybe all of it.

Dave lets him go with a curt nod. Travis gives Dave's shoulder a quick shake, then walks toward the auditorium. He stops at the threshold.

"I kind of wish my dad was here to see me," Travis says. "Going on a rescue mission. Being all manly."

"Thanks for doing this," I say.

Travis shrugs. "Don't thank me too quickly," he says. "I'm doing it for him."

He goes on into the auditorium before I can ask—if I even would—if he's referring to Dave, his father, or someone else.

I look back one last time at the kids in the hallway. Most of them aren't paying any attention to me. Only Dave is watching, mouth set in a determined scowl.

"I'll take care of them," he says.

"I know. Just be fast with that ladder."

"I will."

I follow our team into the auditorium.

Travis and Kenzie hike up the spiral staircase to the grid as Jaime jogs to the scene shop for one of the screwguns. Kat and

Dave will still have one to use to unboard the doors. Chad and I linger at the base of the staircase, waiting for Jaime.

"Hey, dude," Chad says to me as we listen to Jaime searching in the shop.

"What."

"When we get out there . . . try not to kill 'em."

"Right, go for the cripple."

Chad looks me in the eye, and something invisible stabs me hard in the chest. "Naw, man. I mean *you*. You don't kill 'em."

Chad takes a breath through his nose. "It ain't like I thought," he says. "Killin' a person. It ain't nothin' like what I thought. If I get outta here alive, I'm ditchin' the Corps. I don't care if they lock my ten ball up for life, I ain't goin' in."

"You mean that zombie kid outside the library? And the librarian? You didn't have a choice, man. It was them or us. You know what they're capable of. John was right, much as I hate to say it. They're monsters."

Chad shakes his head. "Naw, *you* were right, Brian," he says. "They're still us. I wouldn't be feelin' what I am if it was otherwise."

I shift my weight to square up with him. I keep my voice low. "If one of those motherfuckers is about to hurt Mackenzie—or Laura, or *you*—I'll do whatever I have to do to stop them."

"That's cool," Chad says. "But I'm tellin' you, man, try not to kill anyone. I don't fancy gettin' my ass eaten up today, either, believe me. But you don't want what I got inside me right now. You don't want it. And I ain't talkin' about this infection shit. That's nothin' compared to it. Nothin'."

He slaps my shoulder.

"But I got your back. It comes down to it, you let me take the swing. I'm already screwed."

"You're not screwed, you're—"

Chad grabs the back of my neck and pulls me close.

"Don't shit me, Bri. However long I got, I don't know, but just don't shit me."

I force myself to nod.

Jaime walks across the stage from the scene shop. He's got a tool belt slung around his hips with a screwgun in the holster, like a ray gun straight out of *Star Wars*. Only this gun has a thick drill bit on the end.

"Ready," he says.

We follow him up the stairs, where Travis and Kenzie are waiting by the ladder beneath the trapdoor. Chad starts climbing up first, his bat dangling from his belt. He grimaces with each step, but I think I'm the only one to notice.

"All right," Chad says, breathing hard as he takes hold of the trapdoor handle. "Let's go fuck this monkey."

"Hey, man," I say to Jaime. "Just out of curiosity, is there a Spanish word for zombie?"

Jaime considers this before suggesting: "*Zombrero?*"

And despite everything, we all giggle as Chad opens the trapdoor and climbs out onto the roof. But our laughter comes out sick and distorted. Like it's the last time any of us will ever laugh again.

WE CLIMB UP AFTER CHAD, AND AS SOON AS WE hit the open air, we're wincing. The smell is horrific: rotten meat and piss and burnt hair. Fires still burn brightly from all corners of the city. The parking lot lights are off—they probably only get turned on if there's a play or a game of some kind—but I can see movement, lots of it, between the cars and along the fence. Worse, I can hear them. An insensate moaning chorus bellows up toward us from below, monsters craving our bones.

"*Or* we could go back inside," Travis says, and I'm not sure if he's joking.

Jaime heads over to the air-conditioning unit, where the extension cords we used last time are still tied up. Jaime tests them and nods.

"We're good," he grunts.

As the others start in that direction, Kenzie grabs my hand, pulling me back.

"Brian."

"Yeah."

"You're a part of me. Remember that?"

My heart skips a beat. She said that after she came home from the transplant procedure.

"I know."

"I never told you this before, but . . . I don't think it was the transplant that saved me."

"Of course it wasn't. You were already in remission. The transplant just—"

"I was ready to go," she says. "I really was. I know that's probably hard to believe since I was only nine, but it's true. And then when we found out you matched, you just said yes. Just *said* it. That made me want to fight again. I was so tired, but I wanted to fight for you because you were going to fight for me."

My throat constricts as she speaks, and I turn to watch a fire burn downtown. I don't want her to see my face. My eyes start to burn from forcing them not to blink. If I blink, my whole face will flood.

"Mom will be here," my sister says. "I know she will."

"Yeah. Maybe." I can't think about that right now. I clear my throat and say, "Listen, can you hang off the edge of the awning and drop from there?"

"Sure, I guess so. But—"

"I don't want you in the shit with us if it comes down," I say. And I don't want her to *see* us not surviving a fight, but I won't say that. "Just stay on the awning while we look for Laura. Wait for us to come back this way for the ladder. *Then* you come down, okay? If we don't come back, then climb up the extension cords and go inside."

She starts to argue, but I cut her off. "Do it, Mackenzie."

"Fine," Kenzie says.

"Brian," Travis calls softly. "You coming or what?"

"Love ya, bro," Kenzie says.

"Love ya, sis."

We line up to take turns climbing down to the roof over the

sidewalk. I hug Kenzie, making sure the handle of my Starfire doesn't poke her. I follow after Jaime, landing softly on the angled aluminum roof. Travis comes down next.

I look up, waiting for Chad. He's standing beside my sister, saying something, one hand on her shoulder. After a second, she gives him a hug. I see Chad close his eyes and squeeze her tight, then let her go.

Chad groans as he scales down the cord, the skin on his hands cracking as he clutches it. There's no blood, just a sound like breakfast cereal being stepped on across a tile floor. The rest of us glance at each other, but Chad still appears to be in his right mind.

Chad grits his teeth but refuses to make a sound. God, he must be in so much pain by now.

Kenzie climbs down last. That's everyone.

Jaime looks back to make sure we're all together, then begins inching along the peak of the roof, followed by me, then Travis, then Chad. Kenzie hunkers down beside the wall beneath the auditorium roof.

Focus, I order myself. *Get the job done. Focus on getting the hell out of this school and somewhere safe.*

We go slow, taking our time, not wanting anything below us to hear us moving around. We pass the cafeteria and admin buildings. But halfway along, as we pass the library on the way toward the C buildings, the drama department starts feeling a lot safer. Maybe we *should* stay behind, wait for help. With the doors boarded up good and solid, it's probably the safest place in the entire school right now, and here we are dropping into the unknown, in the dark, not certain if Laura is even—

"We're here," Jaime whispers at me.

I blink. We've arrived at the C buildings.

The A, B, C, and D buildings are all two stories each. Like at the library, the roof we're on is too far from the buildings for us to jump; we'll have to drop down to get into the western C building and then go room to room, upstairs and down.

If Laura understands what we do about the monsters being unable to climb anything easily, then hopefully she's on the second floor. The monsters seem physically capable of climbing stairs, but I hope it'd hurt too much for them to attempt it. Like how they haven't figured a way over the fence yet. But most likely, with those things bearing down on her from the gym, Laura just jumped into the closest classroom she could, shut the door, and hopefully barricaded it with desks or something.

"We're clear below," Jaime whispers. He thumbs the button on his headset, quietly saying Kat's name. He waits. Tries again. Shakes his head.

"Too far out," he says. "We'll have to wait till we're closer to the drama department to signal her."

I nod. Carefully, the four of us dangle from the edge of the awning, then drop down. For one insane moment, I feel truly badass, like a commando.

That moment passes when Chad hits the sidewalk and crumples into a heap, groaning.

"Shit!" Travis hisses. He grabs Chad by the jacket and drags him to the corner of the western C building. Jaime and I scuttle over to both of them, looking around wildly for anything that might have heard. So far, the coast is clear.

"S-sorry," Chad mutters, eyes still shut tight with pain.

"You going to make it?" Jaime demands.

Chad nods. "Yeah. Yeah."

"They'll be coming," I say. "We got to hustle."

Chad climbs to his feet, wincing the entire time. His back is so curled now that he has to rest his forearms on his thighs to stay on his feet. He's taken off Jaime's sling to have the use of both hands. But Mom told him to keep his hand in place, below his heart; what if letting it go speeds up the infection and—

No time to worry about it. We dash along the first-floor row of classrooms. None of them are locked, but all of them are empty.

Goddam it.

I bite my lips between my teeth to keep from screaming Laura's name.

Jaime checks the last classroom, shakes his head, and lets the door shut quietly. I jerk a thumb upward, and Jaime nods. We gather at the base of the stairs and start to go up, but Chad lags behind.

He shakes his head. "Can't."

That's what I figured. And I hate to say it . . . but it's good news for us. If it hurts Chad too much to get up the stairs, then maybe the climb will keep the monsters away too.

"I'll wait here," he says.

I don't hesitate after that. I take the steps two at a time up to the next floor and start pulling doors open. Jaime and Travis do the same, starting at the opposite end of the floor.

"Laura!" I call into each doorway. Jaime gestures for me to be quiet. But I can't, not now; with every empty classroom I get closer and closer to seeing Laura turned into one of those things, like Chad, like Hollis, cramped and hunched and turning into some—

The next door won't quite open.

God, yes, please.

I smash my shoulder into it. It budges about an inch. I throw my entire weight into it and flinch at the cacophony of desks being thrown to the ground.

I push my way through the jumble of upended desks in the dark. Someone—Laura, I pray—must have barricaded herself in here.

Just as I take a breath to call out to Laura in the dark classroom, something smashes into my stomach and sends me sprawling out the door.

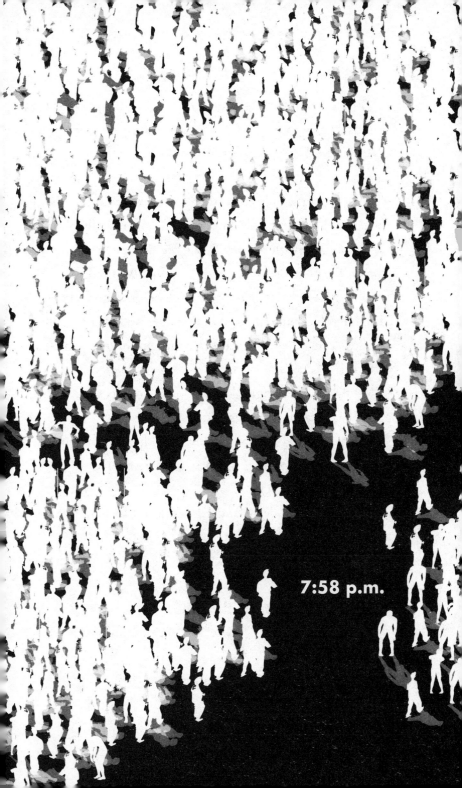

7:58 p.m.

"BRIAN!".

I pull myself into a sitting position, holding my gut. Laura stands in the doorway with a wooden flagpole in her hands. The flag has been ripped off it.

"Laura," I croak.

She drops the pole and rushes to me. "You're okay?" she says, kneeling down and grabbing my arm. "You're really okay?"

I stand up, with her help, trying to breathe into the pain to loosen the knot she's given me. "I'm fine. We need to . . ."

I hesitate as I search her face for blood or wounds. I don't see anything. Her pulse throbs wildly in her neck, her breathing is shallow, eyes wide; all the usual symptoms of one of her panic attacks.

Only . . . she's not shaking. And she's on her feet.

"Are you all right?" I ask quickly.

"Fine," she says. "I ran in here from the gym when they . . . God, what's happening? All these people were like—"

"You're not panicking?"

"I'm scared to death and I'd rather not be here right now, but no."

I don't have time to talk about it, but this is last thing I expected from her.

"Are we going home?" she asks.

"We're going to try," I say. "Where are your meds?"

"My meds . . . ?"

"Your drugs, your panic stuff, where is it?"

"In my bag."

I hear footsteps. Echoing from some nearby part of the school.

Running. Scraping. Like crystals over concrete.

Travis races past me toward the stairs, sword aloft. "It's on," he says.

I go to the railing and look down. Six students—former students—on all fours are gunning full-tilt toward Chad, who's still at the bottom of the stairs, back bent, bat raised.

"Go, go, go!" Jaime screams at me, following Travis down the steps.

I turn to Laura. "Get your bag. We need your pills, and we need them now."

"Brian, a little help!" Travis shouts.

Laura shakes her head like there's too much happening. "But my bag's in the gym."

Oh, god*dam* it.

"Come on," I say, pulling her toward the stairs. "We have to get those pills."

"Brian, what—"

"It's the only way to try to help Chad. He's sick. Now stay behind me."

She doesn't ask questions. I almost trip going down the dusty concrete steps but keep my feet under me and skid to a halt behind Travis and Jaime.

"Bring it!" Chad bellows as the six zombies gallop toward him. Then he coughs, that same wet, hacking cough Hollis had this morning. He spits yellow sludge on the concrete.

I drop Laura's hand and put mine on the handle of my sword. As the last of the six passes under the awning, someone dives from the awning behind the monster. A flash of something maroon slaps over the zombie's head, disorienting it.

"*Kenzie?*"

"Watch out!" Kenzie shouts as the zombie she's blinded with her overshirt tears the cloth off its head and continues to rampage in our direction.

Here we go.

8:01 p.m.

THE FIRST ZOMBIE REACHES CHAD. HE LIMPS toward the monster, this white girl in a tight blue miniskirt and tan blouse, her face grotesque, saliva swinging from her misshapen mouth. She leaps; Chad swings.

The bat catches her in midflight, slamming into her neck. I almost expect her head to get hammered off, but it doesn't. The blow disrupts her trajectory, and she careens ass over elbows into the sidewalk. She's slow to get up.

Still—it's a victory, and it flushes adrenaline through my body.

"Yes!" I shout, knowing it's a bad idea, knowing it will only draw more creatures this way, but unable to stop myself. Kenzie dashes toward a classroom door but doesn't go inside; she crouches down, hands balled into fists, watching the fight begin.

I can't believe she came down here. I told her stay, I *told* her . . .

As the zombies rush us, Laura breaks away, tearing back up the stairs. Probably for the best. Safer.

I turn back to the zombies. Chad chokes down on the bat with both hands.

"*It's Chad o'clock, motherfuckers!*" he howls, and even though I'm about to fight for my life, I start laughing my ass off. Laughing, or shrieking.

Chad thunders down the sidewalk toward the next two closest monsters, a black girl and a white boy. They bound toward him, their crystalline arms sparkling beneath the overhead sidewalk lights. Yelping wildly, they close in on my best friend.

I run to Chad. He clocks the white boy solidly on the skull, sending him skidding into the wall, jaundiced eyes rolling in his head. Before I can even reach Chad, he re-cocks his arms and fires the business end of his weapon at the black girl. Her head snaps backward, taking her feet out from under her.

Jaime appears beside me, and Travis rushes closer as the other three monsters ignore their fallen buddies.

"We gotta move!" Jaime shouts, but stands in place and raises his Starfire.

"The gym!" I yell back. "The meds are in the gym!"

No one answers. Chad breaks left, picking out the largest of the three monsters. I circle a white guy in jock apparel. Jaime swears and breaks right toward a Latina girl—the flesh of her right shin is torn and mangled, and it hits me this is the same girl we saw outside the auditorium. One of her front teeth is missing.

Chad dodges his attacker, pivots, and swings for the back of the monster's head. The monster spins to attack from another angle, and the bat whiffs past him. Chad dances painfully away, keeping the bat between him and the kid, but the kid is relentless, growling and swiping his inflamed hand at Chad's legs. Chad swings the bat, catching the monster in the face. In the time it takes the monster to shake off the blow, Chad brings the bat down in a beautiful arc square on the monster's crown, sending him flat.

The girl jumps toward Jaime, mouth wide, preparing to bite. Jaime sticks the sword out with one hand, but it's a flimsy grip, and the girl's weight knocks the weapon out of Jaime's grasp. Jaime pinwheels his arms, backing up as she closes on him. She pounces. Jaime goes down, screwgun clattering out of the holster. They wrestle, the girl trying to pin Jaime's shoulders and snapping her jaws at his face as her spit dribbles down Jaime's skin.

Then from behind me, Laura rushes past, lifting the flagpole high over head. She's screaming and, I think, crying at the same time. She runs straight at the girl on top of Jaime and brings the pole down on her back. Again. Again.

This gets the girl's attention away from Jaime for a split second. Jaime's right hand scrambles for the screwgun; he finds it, presses the trigger, and jams the drill bit into the girl's ribs.

The bit sings a soprano whine, then gurgles as it digs into her flesh and bone. Jaime screams madly while driving the bit deeper into her ribs. The girl gives an unearthly screech and tries to pull away from the screwgun. Jaime grabs her by the blouse and shoves her onto her back. Now he's on top, shouting obscenities in her face while the drill bit digs deeper and deeper.

Distantly, I hear Laura screaming, "Oh my god! Oh my god!" over and over.

I fight the urge to turn to her as the jock leaps at me.

Don't kill 'em.

Cursing, I drop low and swing hard for his legs. The sword

cracks against the kid's shin. He stumbles over the sword, but gets right back to his hands and knees, roaring. I lash out with one foot. Feel the sole of my shoe squish against his swollen lower lip. The blow sends him to his back.

Go for the cripple.

I jump toward him and chop down with the Starfire like an ax against his knees. There's a brittle crack. As the kid lurches up to reach for me, I swing again, connecting with his other knee.

I skip backward. The kid flips over, dragging himself toward me on his hands, his legs motionless behind him. I fight the urge to clip him in the head. He's slowed; it'll do. Desperately, I swing my head in search of Kenzie and Laura. Kenzie's still by the classroom door, and there's Laura, beside her, holding the pole out in front of her like a spear. The other zombies don't seem to notice them yet.

Travis appears beside the kid I just hit. He raises his sword and swings at the monster's head. The resulting gash spills crimson blood against the dirty sidewalk, and the monster lies still.

Absurdly, Travis stares down at the monster and says, almost calmly, "I'm sorry, man."

Chad races to Jaime and swings at the Latina girl like his bat was a golf club, smashing her cheekbone into a pulpy mass. Blood sprays across Jaime's face. He shrieks and jumps off her lifeless body, wiping frantically at his skin and spitting.

I turn to Laura and hold out my hand. "Come on!"

Laura's ponytail has come undone. Her hair spills around her face, and for one second, I'm reminded of how she looks after we've been making out for an hour. She is so beautiful.

Laura runs over to me but refuses my hand, still holding the pole. "Can we just—"

Another monster, a thin white kid wearing all black, runs around the corner of the building. I pull Laura close and force her to run alongside me, racing for the gymnasium.

"This way!" I call out to the guys.

They steer toward me. Jaime stops only long enough to pick up his Starfire. Chad screams in agony as he lurches toward the gymnasium.

"Hurry up, hurry up," Jaime chants as the monster closes in.

I drop Laura's arm and throw open both doors.

"Oh, my sweet chocolaty hell," Travis whispers.

We've only seen maybe a hundred sick kids from the roof, total. There are probably more out on the fields, and maybe survivors trapped or hiding in classrooms.

But a lot of the school was in the gym for the pep rally, and they were there when we went on lockdown. Everyone who did what they were told, like nice little students, ended up here.

They're *still* here.

What's left of them.

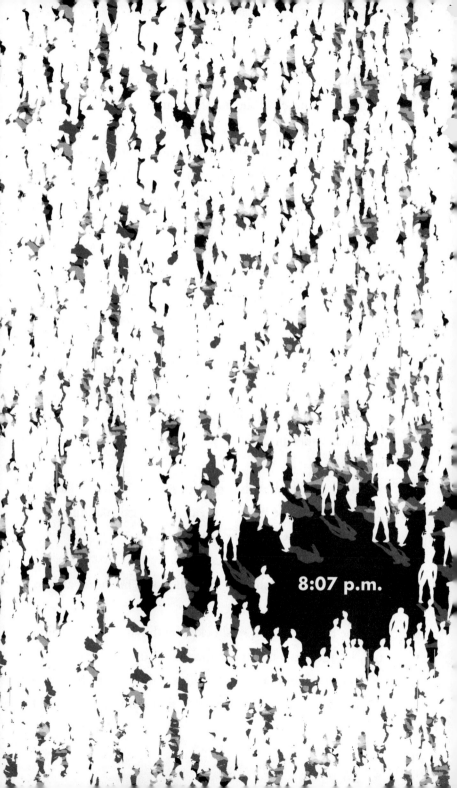
8:07 p.m.

CARNAGE.

I can't see much of the polished hardwood floor. The bodies are too thick, too piled, too many. At my feet, I recognize two of the delta-bravo football players in matching jerseys we passed this morning when Frank the security guard hassled us. Not sick and dead. Just dead. Somehow they look younger now.

Wandering among the bodies are the *walking* dead, the monsters, at least thirty at a quick mental count. Maybe more. They crawl around on their knees and hands like the others, faces malformed and drooping, arms swollen and brittle.

The zombies, one at a time, turn their heads toward us. Their movements are slow, lethargic.

And on the opposite side of the gym, beyond the horde, resting against the wall, I see Laura's bubble-gum pink backpack.

"Son of a bitch," I whisper. "Son of a *bitch*."

Jaime wipes his mouth with the back of his hand. "You wanna . . ."

I look at Chad as the zombies stare us down. Chad's eyes flicker between the bag and the creatures, calculating.

"Well, shit," Chad says. "Maybe if—"

"*Brian, down!*" Kenzie screeches.

I drop to a crouch. A zombie flies over my head, arms outstretched.

The thin kid. I was so shocked by the sight in the gymnasium, I forgot he was still out there behind us, charging.

The zombie smashes into Jaime, taking them both down. This cues the others in the gym to start rampaging toward us.

Travis guts the zombie on top of Jaime with a fast stab of his sword. Jaime clambers up, breathing hard, and turns to me.

"Brian, I don't . . . I don't think . . ."

"I know," I say.

And we turn to start running out of the gym, leaving behind our only hope for Chad.

Thirty, forty creatures stumble over the bodies of the dead to reach us. Students of every color, every grade, every clique are running at us. They roar collectively, and I swear I feel the ground shake beneath me.

From the sky, they'd look like swarming ants.

"Holy Mary," Jaime whispers, "Mother of G—"

Travis shoves him, and then we're through the doorway and back onto the main sidewalk. Jaime slams the doors shut behind us.

A tremendous crash rattles the gym doors. I wonder crazily why the hell they couldn't figure out how to open the doors and let themselves out. Maybe we wasted time boarding up the drama department. Come to think of it, none had grabbed any doorknobs or handles, just crashed into the doors. It would be funny if it wasn't so goddam stupid.

"Okay, let's go, move it," Chad urges as we sprint down the main sidewalk. His pace is slowing, though. He's moving as best he can, but now it's clear he doesn't have much longer.

Chad. Hang in there, man.

As if he can hear my thoughts, Chad glances at me. I've slowed down just a bit, unconsciously, to stay at his side.

"Chad, what's wrong?" Laura says as we move down the sidewalk. Her voice is high, tight, her eyes wide. But she's under control.

"You get them outta here," Chad says raggedly, ignoring Laura. "No matter what. You do whatever you gotta to get them out."

I don't say anything.

My breath scorches out of my lungs like fire. Chad bellows with every step, swearing painfully as the disease continues to overtake him.

A splintering crash echoes behind us, and we shudder to a stop. Whatever kept the monsters penned inside the gym, they're out now. They've smashed the doors open, and they pour out in a flood of vicious hunger.

The stampede is bearing down right on us, maybe forty yards back.

Without a word, we pick up our pace. But Chad still lags behind, wincing and swearing with every step. He is almost entirely curled over now.

A crash and clang sound behind me. I glance back; Travis has tripped and is splayed across the concrete.

We all stumble to a halt.

"Travis!" Jaime shouts.

But the horde is closer now, rolling toward us in an inevitable wave. Eyes bulging, flesh hanging, jaws snapping. My American history teacher is one of them. The security guard who stopped us this morning is another. They weren't in the gym—the noise of the horde must've attracted them from someplace else on campus as we ran. Swelling their ranks.

The sight of them closing in paralyzes us for one precious moment as Travis shoves himself to his feet.

Chad spins toward us. The skin under his eyes has begun to bag and slough. The first tints of yellow have appeared at the corners. His hands shake uncontrollably.

"*Go!*" Chad orders.

"We gotta get Travis!" I scream back.

"I got it," Chad says. "Just go." He snorts and grins. "Few and the proud, right?"

His eyes dart to my sister. He actually manages to wink at her and smile. "Love ya, Kenzie," he says.

Then he turns to face the onslaught.

I reach out to stop him. I can't let my friend go out like this, not for that queer-ass Travis—he's dead anyway.

For a split second, I lose my breath entirely. *Jesus-I-really-just-thought-that-oh-god-what's-happened-to-me-what's—*

"*Chad!*"

Too late. He whirls away and books toward Travis.

Travis retrieves his sword. Chad gets to him and shoves him back our way. Travis needs no more encouragement, and he races toward us.

One monster, faster than the others, reaches Chad first. He snarls and lands on top of Chad, sending Chad to the ground once more. The monster grips Chad's good hand and buries his teeth into the scabby flesh.

With a barbaric howl, Chad kicks the zombie off of him. He reaches for his bat and drives it into the kid's mouth. Cussing, Chad skitters backward and clambers to his feet as six more zombies race toward him on their toes and knuckles, dotting the sidewalk with slick saliva.

Then the horde slows. Just for a moment. Several of the monsters sniff at Chad's leg—then refocus on us and give chase again.

Chad turns. His eyes are wide as he registers what this means. He drops the bat, digs into his jeans, and throws his car keys at me like a fastball. Stupidly, I try to grab at them with my sword still in hand, and they clatter to the sidewalk.

"*Run!*" Chad screams. His lower lip now juts out from his face, and I can see even from this distance that his eyes have gone yellow.

Then Laura is on the ground, swooping the keys into her hand. She faces me, terrified, but not panicked.

"Brian . . . ?"

"Okay," I whisper, and we turn and run for the parking lot.

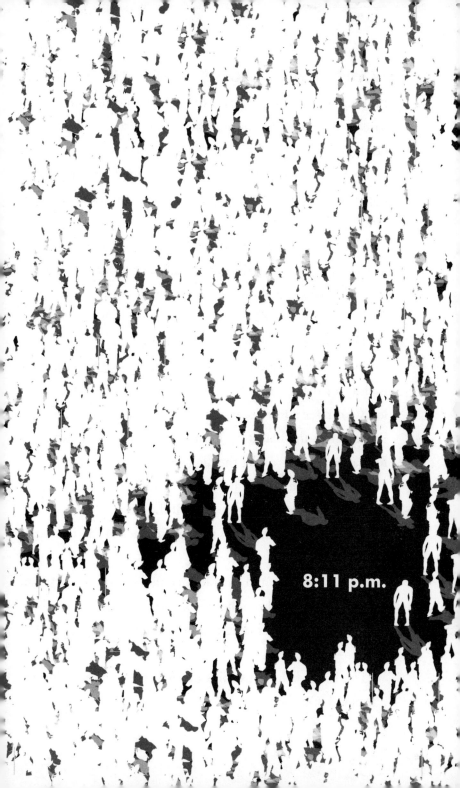

"KAT!" JAIME SHOUTS INTO THE HEADSET, running awkwardly with his sword in one hand and the headset base in the other, his thumb down on the send button. "We need the ladder *now*."

Over the sound of the monsters, I can't tell if she replies or not. Then a heartbeat later, Jaime calls over his shoulder, "Box office!"

The ladder is a thirty-footer. It would be a mess to try to maneuver it around in the drama hallway. From the box office doors, it'll be a straight shot across the parking lot.

If we make it that far.

The horde closes in. We run toward the parking lot, instinctively veering east, away from the scene shop. Our way is clear for the moment, but as soon as we hit the edge of the lot, we can see a few dozen monsters roaming among the cars. Bodies litter the blacktop, most with their throats and arms torn apart, rotting under the night sky.

I point to the gate. "The hoods. Of those two cars. Can use them to get a leg up over the fence if the ladder—"

"Right," Jaime says. Into the headset, he barks, "Kat, head for the gate."

He bends down and runs in a crouch toward the first car, and the rest of us follow. The zombies marauding in the parking lot haven't seen us yet. There's a chance we can sneak our way to the—

The horde behind us spills out into the lot, bellowing for our blood. Our bones.

Peeking around the closest car, I see the other zombies perk up and start moving toward their mutated brothers and sisters.

This is bad.

"I really do hate being manly," Travis says with a wild look on his face. Before I can react, he bolts away from us, running upright, all six feet of him. At first I'm pissed, thinking he's just looking out for himself. Then I realize the horde can see him more clearly than us, and half of them break into their apelike run after him.

He's leading them away from us.

I reach for Jaime to point this out to him, but he's already moving around the front of the car to dash to the next one for cover. I pull Laura and Kenzie around the rear of the vehicle.

I guessed better than Jaime.

One of the parking lot monsters is headed straight for him. Jaime stops, looks around for an escape.

It takes Jaime too long. That's all the time the monster needs to jump and take Jaime to the ground. The screwgun flies out of his hand, just out of reach, and the monster sinks his teeth into Jaime's throat.

With an earsplitting cry, Laura breaks free from me and charges full-bore toward the zombie on top of Jaime, her flagpole in both hands, the brass knob at the top pointed at the creature. She sticks the zombie square in the ribs, making him tumble off Jaime. Laura is screaming incoherently now—words, I think, but I can't make them out. It's as if she's released all her years of fear onto this one creature.

The zombie regains his footing and turns to leap at her.

As he scrambles over Jaime, Jaime manages to grab the screwgun and jam it up into the zombie's belly. The bit drills deep, hurling flesh from the spinning corkscrew. The zombie falls across him, creating an obscene cross of their two bodies.

Laura jabs the flagpole into the zombie's head over and over. It's not having much effect, but it's keeping him busy. I rush over to her and shove the zombie off Jaime just as the drill bit pops through the creature's skin near its spine. At last the monster stops moving.

Laura, breathing hard, drops the pole and covers her face with her hands. Kenzie joins us as I bend down to check Jaime's wound. He's still depressing the trigger on the screwgun; its keening wail burning my ears.

"Jaime," I whisper urgently.

His eyes roll toward me. "Asa," he wheezes, and a fresh glut of blood pours from the wound in his neck. "Madison . . ."

"We'll try, man . . ."

A blood bubble forms and pops on Jaime's lips, and his muscles go limp. All except for his right hand, which even now holds down the trigger on the screwgun. The bit catches on the blacktop and sends sparks into the air.

"I'm sorry," I hear myself say.

"We gotta get out of here," Kenzie urges.

Gritting my teeth, I pull Laura's hands away from her face. "Come on," I say, and pull her into a crouching run to the next vehicle. I think of Kat. She'll never get that second kiss.

Kat . . .

I spin toward the school, searching. There! Kat and Dave are holding the ladder sideways, running as best they can toward the gate. The ladder bangs against their legs. Dave is scanning the lot fearfully, but Kat's face is set in a determined scowl. The horde—most of them, anyway—haven't noticed the two of them yet; they're too focused on us or have chased after Travis. Another few seconds, though, and Kat and Dave will be in the zombies' line of sight.

We move ahead to the next vehicle. Now we're maybe ten, fifteen cars away from the gate. Bill the security guard is still splayed across the trunk of one car, motionless and pale, colossal gashes in his forearms encrusted with blood.

I jerk on Laura's hand, urging her to follow quickly to the next car, a little two-door thing. I stop at the rear bumper.

Damon's car. I recognize the white peace decal.

Damon's car. *Damon's gun.*

I scuttle around toward the driver's side. It's definitely Damon's, because Damon is crouched beside the door, pawing uselessly at the handle with his enormous, crystallized club hands.

He turns. Our eyes meet. His lower lip distends past his smooth white chin, teeth jagged. A low growl rumbles deep in his chest.

I swing the Starfire low at the same time Damon lunges toward me.

The sword clips Damon's shoulder, sending him facedown

into the blacktop. I hear crystals snapping as his chest hits the ground. He stretches out his arms, trying to get back up.

I kneel and chop with the sword, aiming for his arm. The blade connects solidly with Damon's wrist. There's a snap, and his hand arches upward as the bones in his wrist give way. Damon doesn't even notice, still trying to push himself up. I chop again, against his other hand.

It takes three whacks before his wrist breaks. Damon falls to the ground, too stupid-crazy to use his legs to get up.

Still alive. Good. Just like Chad said . . .

"They're coming!" Kenzie shrieks.

I shove Damon away from the driver's side door and open it, thanking god it's not locked. I reach under the seat—and there it is, cold and heavy. A pistol.

I pull it out and yank off the nylon holster. A revolver. Six-shooter, I guess. I turn it over in my hands for a couple of seconds, assuming there's a safety. I find a latch on one side, click it, and seem to know from years of Hollywood training that this is now a live gun. I accidentally hit a button with my thumb, and a dot of red light dances on the side of the car.

Six shots. If it's loaded.

I turn back to the girls. "Run," I say. "The gate—go, now."

They don't hesitate. Laura and Kenzie bolt for the gate as I stand up and survey our situation.

While most of the gym monsters have followed Travis around the west end of the performing arts department, there are still dozens of them in the parking lot. It only takes a second for one to spot me and start bolting in my direction, wailing for my flesh.

I break into a sprint, the gun in my right hand.

"*Move!*" I scream.

Kenzie and Laura reach the gate at the same time as Kat and Dave. With one mighty heave, Kat tosses the narrow end of the ladder onto the crossbeam of the fence. Dave drops his end to the ground. Now we have a stepped ramp to climb up. Dave gestures hurriedly to Kat, who starts scrambling up the ladder.

Kenzie lets out a wail as she brushes one of Bill's dead arms.

"Brian, come on!" Laura cries.

Both girls are already standing on one of the hoods. Kenzie has the fence in both hands as she tries to pull herself up and over, too intent on getting to safety to think about going for the ladder. I get a quick image of her slipping, impaling herself on those goddam spikes, and this is enough to send me running again.

"The ladder, the ladder," I say, panting.

Laura jumps toward the ladder and tries to hoist herself onto it rather than climb from the base. I swear and get beneath her, pushing one foot until she can get her legs onto it. My heart seizes as she balances for one precarious moment on top of the ladder. Then she skitters along the rungs to the top of the fence and leaps, landing on the other side.

Thank you, God.

Dave goes next as Kat hollers at him to hurry from the sidewalk on the other side of the fence. But his feet slip, and one leg shoots between the rungs on the ladder, wishboning him. Dave grunts, cusses, and tries to extricate himself.

But now he's blocking the way for my sister. I jump onto the hood beside Kenzie and shove her as she tries to climb the fence.

"Go, go," I chant at her, pushing her ass up.

A hand grapples for my foot. I spin and kick out. The zombie kid takes the shot in the shoulder and spins away from us.

When I look past him, my guts clench again and I wonder if I just shit myself.

A swarm of diseased living dead is rushing for us. They clamber over one another, hunched and starved, lurching toward us in a relentless flood.

We have maybe ten seconds.

"Kenzie, please," I whisper, because my chest is so tight with fear I can't scream anymore.

Kenzie puts two hands on the fence. Laura, temporarily safe on the other side, urges her to keep going. Kenzie pushes down to boost herself up, but her strength fails, and she slides down to the hood again. Dave is completely tangled in the ladder now, twisting his hips, his legs, trying to get back onto it proper.

I fire the gun into the throng. My ears ring with the report. A white chick spins and falls, causing three other monsters to stumble over her. But all four of them recover quickly; the bullet caught the girl in the stomach, and it barely slows her.

"Kenzie, *go*," I say, and my voice is muffled in my own ears.

"I *can't*!"

I crouch down and put my left shoulder under her ass and shove.

"*Go!*"

The keening from the zombies increases, puncturing my deafness. Kenzie squeals, then manages to get her feet on the top crossbar. She's hunched over, grasping the spikes in both hands to steady herself. Her legs quake.

I'm grateful for all those days of ditching; my muscle reflex kicks in, and I'm up and over the fence in less than a moment, landing in a heap beside my girlfriend.

I made it! I shriek in my head, or at least I think it's in my head. *I made it, you bastards, I'm safe!*

Kenzie screams.

A high-pitched, heart-searing cry that punches through my chest.

I spin back toward the gate as Laura cries out. Dave thumps to the ground beside her, finally free from the ladder.

Kenzie has slipped off the fence. She's on the hood again, on the school side of the fence, the monster side. *Why doesn't she try to jump again?* I wonder stupidly. The zombies are only a few feet away, clawing at one another to reach her.

That's when I see the fence has punctured her left arm, pinning her in place. Blood runs down the fence post beneath the limb. Red flows down the white bars. School colors.

The zombies reach the fence.

And Chad is in the lead.

Awesome! I think deliriously. *If anyone can get Kenzie over the side in one piece, it's—*

Kenzie screams my name, eyes wide. She's trying to use her right hand to pry her left arm off the spike, but she can't make herself do it.

Chad reaches the hood in front of the horde.

His face—

Arms—

Oh, god, no.

My best friend, now utterly one of Them, grabs my sister by the back of the pants and hoists himself up to her, teeth bared, lip fat and drooping. He swings his other swollen, encrusted hand to grab Kenzie's long hair, using it to pull himself toward her.

"Brian, help me!"

The zombie cocks his head back, thrusts it forward to her neck.

My mouth falls slack as I raise the gun and pull the trigger.

8:16 p.m.

CHAD FALLS AWAY FROM KENZIE, LANDING facedown on the car, arms and legs splayed.

I scuttle for my Starfire and shove it between the bars and onto the hood of the car. I scramble recklessly back over the fence, dropping beside Kenzie.

Our problem just got a lot bigger, my brilliant plan backfiring in our faces: the ladder is still in place, creating easy access for the monsters to get free from the school, over the fence, and target Laura, Dave, and Kat.

"Kenzie," I say over the roar of the oncoming horde. "Look at me."

Kenzie does, eyes narrow with pain.

Before I can stop to think about it, I grab her arm in both hands and yank it up. The sound it makes twists my guts into knots.

Kenzie's mouth falls open, but the pain must be so intense that it cuts off her air. She doesn't make a sound—not at first. A heartbeat later, staring at the blood cascading down her arm, she releases a cry of exquisite agony.

No time.

I drop the pistol to the hood, pick her up in my arms, and find the adrenalized strength to toss her onto the ladder. Despite her wound, Kenzie crawls up and falls to the other side of the fence. When she sits up, holding her wounded arm to her chest, I nod once, to myself. She'll be fine, for the moment.

The horde is closing in. Clawed hands and jaundiced eyes

seek my marrow. I start to grab for the fence when I see the last thing I expected.

The stagecraft kids. All of them, by the looks of it. Pouring out of the box office doors and running full speed toward me.

Then those in the vanguard—led by John, who is running as if he doesn't care one bit if anyone else is following—come to a halt when they see the zombies stretching toward me.

They'll never get through this many zombies and to the ladder. And they know it. But their panic at seeing the wreckage of bodies in the lot, the horde in front of me, and freedom so close . . . not a single one of them makes to run back to the box office, where it would be safer.

Or maybe they're wondering if anyone will ever come back for them.

I focus on the zombies coming closer.

All right, fuckers. All right, then.

I grab the collar of Chad's leather jacket and pull. It whisks off with surprising ease. Like he's handing it to me. I try hard not to hear the sound his mutilated face makes when it slaps against the hood again. A beat later, his body slides to the blacktop.

I pull Chad's jacket on, shrug into it so it falls just right, and zip it up to the collar.

Then I pick up the pistol in my right hand, the sword in my left.

I take a wide stance on the hood of the car, face the zombies, and scream.

"Come on!"

The four monsters closest to me drop dead when I shoot them in the face, aided by the laser sight of Damon's gun. When the cylinder dry-fires on the next round, empty, I let the pistol drop and jump off the hood.

I charge at the monsters, swinging the Starfire with both hands, cutting a path to meet the stagecraft kids in the middle. There's no skill involved. I'm no warrior. I just swing right, left, right, left, cursing and screaming until my breath burns like fire. I aim high every time, slamming the sword against as many heads as I can. Screw Chad's order to go for the cripple. These things aren't human anymore . . .

There's no shortage of targets. Every swing connects somewhere, against someone. Every hit moves one monster out of the way or drops it flat. I fill the space and swing again, and again, and again.

A crash over by the auditorium catches my ear. I pivot in the middle of a swing to see what's going on and notice two figures on the roof.

Then I see one zombie drop as a lighting instrument smashes into his back.

I risk a prolonged look and see Serena and Tara cheering themselves. A moment later, they chuck two more lights. One smashes uselessly against a car; the other trips up a zombie.

I scream incoherently and start swinging my sword again. The two of them may as well be the cavalry.

I imagine hearing tires squeal down the street behind me in

the distance. Fevered dreams of Green Berets or Army Rangers flash in the back of my mind as I swing. Swing. *Swing . . .*

John and the others break from their paralysis and run toward the ladder. The zombies, uninterested in climbing anything when they have me to feed on, pay no attention as the other students start going up the ladder in a human chain. A few monsters catch sight of them and begin to grab but are kicked away long enough for people to keep climbing.

Yes! I think. *They're gonna make it.*

A guy falls beneath my sword. Then a girl. But my arms are heavy now, tired. My lungs feel like they're going to collapse any second. I can't keep up this pace, and they just keep coming . . .

A bellow resounds through the parking lot. I spin, blink to make sure I'm not still imagining things, then burst into exhausted laughter as Travis and Cammy appear from around the side of drama building, weapons raised. They charge into the mass of the infected, maybe five yards away from me, swinging hard. Zombies fall beneath their blows, and for several heartbeats, it almost looks as if they are dropping two, three monsters at a time. The monsters are falling so rapidly around them, it's as if their weapons are enchanted.

The sight of them gives me one last burst of energy, and I slam my Starfire into some girl's stomach, one of the prissy cheerleaders.

The bodies are piling up now. I swing for another kid, open a gash on his scalp, and then fall backward over some dead thing, some body.

Before I can get up, another infected kid jumps toward me, mouth open, teeth glittering, bone sticking out from his arm. Keith.

I figure he'll be the last thing I see as I hear a thousand voices screaming my name into the cold November air.

All right, I hear myself think. *This is it. This is how it ends.*

8:18 p.m.

SUDDENLY KEITH ROCKETS BACKWARD, LANDING

in a jumbled pile, his sneakered feet twitching.

"This way!" someone shouts from behind me. From the fence.

I pick myself up to half-sitting position, leaning back on my hands. Something is ringing in my ears. Then I hear another gunshot, and another kid goes down.

I look back toward the fence. Two cops are shooting between the bars, picking kids off one by one. I see my mother behind him, holding Kenzie and Laura to her beside her car, her face drawn and strained.

Mom.

"Come on, come on!" one of the cops shouts.

I didn't imagine it, I think stupidly. Some of the zombies around Cammy and Travis—they were shot by the cops.

I try to pull myself up but can't. I let go of the Starfire and try again, but it's no good. Too exhausted, too spent.

Then Cammy is standing in front of me, holding out a hand.

"Hurry," she says, panting. "There's more coming."

I take her hand. Cammy pulls me to my feet, and we dart around lifeless bodies to get to the two cars crashed in front of the gate. Travis is already there, battling a handful of zombies lurching for him. From around the east corner of the drama department, a fresh wave of the infected races at us. The creatures from the gym. Travis must've led them on a chase all over campus.

One of the cops swears and adjusts his position to assist Travis. He pumps three rounds into the crowd, then hurries to reload.

Cammy hops onto the ladder and climbs easily over the fence. I grab Travis by the collar to urge him to follow.

Travis hauls himself onto the hood of one of the cars and tosses himself carelessly onto the ladder, then on over the fence. I look up at the auditorium roof; Serena is waving both arms, a shadowy figure outlined against the burnt orange sky. I raise a weak hand, not sure if she can see me do it, then hike the ladder and drop over the fence.

I hit the ground ass-first, which hurts, but I barely register it. Laura and Kat pull me by my shoulders a safe distance away just as the second wave of zombies hits the fence, growling and reaching for us. Hollis is there among them, his blue shirt starched and cracked with old blood.

Travis, tall sucker that he is, runs to the fence, lifts the narrow end of the ladder off the crossbar, and pushes hard. The ladder bobbles up off the fence, then clatters to the parking lot.

"Brian!" my mom cries.

Laura helps me to my feet, and I stumble over to my mother. She wraps me in a hug.

"Thank god, thank god," she says, over and over, squeezing me so tight I almost lose my breath.

"You should sit down," Laura says.

I nod, and Mom leads me to the sidewalk on the opposite

side of Scarlet. She pulls a cylinder of antibacterial wipes from her car and starts cleaning my face. For a moment, I'm five years old and she's wiping my nose free of allergy snot. But when I open my eyes during the pause it takes her to grab a fresh one, I see nothing but red and black on the cloth. Blood. Sweat. God knows what else.

"Water," I croak.

"Oh, of course," Mom says, and reaches into the car again. She hands me a warm bottle of water and says, "Wash your mouth out first. My god, you're a wreck. I should make you gargle with peroxide."

Who knows if she's kidding. I do as she says, rinsing the tang of blood and salt of grime out of my mouth. I wonder if I'll ever taste anything else. Once the worst is out and I down the water, I almost throw it back up.

"Infected?" I say.

Mom arches an eyebrow, now cleaning off my neck and hands.

"Am I?" I say. "Because of . . . the blood . . ."

Mom scrubs harder. "It's unlikely," she says. "But I'm not taking any chances. We'll do the best decon we can, then run tests and make sure. But you're probably okay. Were you bitten?"

I shake my head, only nominally sure I haven't been. Mom pauses in her cleanup to hug me again.

Once she's satisfied with my skin, she moves to tend to Kenzie while barking questions and orders at the stagecraft kids. I sink to the pavement and lie back, trying to catch my breath, staring at the smoky sky. My eyes shut.

I lose track of time for a long while. I don't pass out; I can hear the monsters in the parking lot moaning and keening for us, hear their mutated arms cracking against the bars.

Finally I open my eyes. I'm still on the ground, on my back. The night sky is pale gray, and only the brightest stars poke their light through the gloom.

Laura is kneeling beside me. Her hair hangs limp around her chin, tangled and clumped.

She takes my hand in both of hers and begins to cry. Quietly.

"Looks like we got survivors on the roof," one of the deputies says.

"And in the school," Kenzie tells him.

I lift my head, wincing, and watch Mom wrap Kenzie's arm in gauze. Both of their faces are ghastly pale. Mom reaches into her medical bag and prepares a slender syringe with something from a bottle.

"We'll take care of it," the first deputy says.

"How?" I ask him. My voice is still dry and rusty despite the water

"Tear gas has been working," he says. "They might not feel much, but they still need to breathe. We've had some luck with Tasers and beanbag shots. We'll get them." He's watching the fence as he says all this, and rubs his mouth with one hand. "Jesus, what a mess."

Mom jabs the needle into Kenzie's arm. Kenzie's either so

used to needles or her arm hurts so much that she doesn't seem to notice.

Mom rubs the spot, somehow frowning and smiling at the same time the way only a mom can. "That'll take care of the pain for now, baby," she says. "We'll get you all patched up as soon as the hospitals are open again."

"Might be a while," the deputy mutters.

Mom shoots him a look, and the deputy motions to his partner. They approach the fence but don't get too close. Then they spot Tara's dad and move toward him, checking for signs of life. Some distant part of my brain is glad that Tara hasn't made it out yet. That it'll be someone else's job to tell her about him.

Mom returns to her car and comes back with a thermos. She pours out some coffee, which has lost most of its steam. Laura helps me into a sitting position as Mom hands me the cup. I take a sip, which at least replaces the worst of the gory taste in my mouth, but that's all I can stomach. I hold it back out for someone to take, and Kenzie, Travis, and Cammy approach us.

Travis gestures to the thermos. "Mind?" he asks.

I shake my head. He pours himself a cup and drinks it down at once. Cammy does the same. The rest of the stagecraft students, who stay huddled together on the far sidewalk, watch enviously, but even John's not dumb enough to demand some for himself.

"Never seen anything like it," Travis says.

"No," I say, as my eyelids begin to fall. It takes an effort to open them.

"I mean you," Travis says. "In the lot. Man, you were going to town."

I say nothing. From where I'm sitting on the sidewalk, I can see Chad's bare, crystalline arm draped across the blacktop. It dawns on me I'm still wearing my best friend's leather jacket.

"Why'd you come back?" Cammy asks. "You were free and clear."

"Why did you?" I say, drawing myself further into Chad's jacket.

"Because we saw you out here," Cammy replies. "That's all. Couldn't let one of my boys slug it out alone."

Alone.

That word vibrates in my skull, rattles my brain. I've got my sister, my mom, my girl. And I've never felt so alone in my whole life.

What did I do?

Kenzie seems to sense my thoughts. She puts a hand over mine. "He would have killed me," she whispers. "You had to do it. I'm so sorry, Brian."

A thousand and one action movies unspool in my mind, starring me as the Hero: ways I could have tried to save everyone, ways I could have done something—or everything—different. When the credits roll on the last one, I realize Kenzie's right.

Travis and Cammy glance at each other and silently move off to one side. Laura hugs me close.

"Thank you," she whispers.

I nod. It's about all I have the strength left for. "How did you . . . I thought you'd be catatonic," I say.

"I came pretty close," Laura says. "But they've been having me taper off the meds. That's what I was going to tell you. I've been doing a little better."

I remember the way she didn't hesitate to belt me in the stomach when I opened the classroom door. How she acted to help Jaime.

"A lot better," I say. "You were really brave."

"And you came looking for me. Thank you." Laura smiles through fresh tears and wraps her arms around me.

Mom comes back with more bottles of water. They're a little warm from being in the trunk of her car, but I don't care. I open a new bottle and slosh half of it down. I taste less blood and dirt. But it's still there. Maybe I'm imagining it.

"Mom?" I say. "There's no cure, right?"

Mom touches my arm. "No, sweetie," she says. "Not yet. We might find one, or at least a treatment, but it'll be a long time coming."

"Good."

"Good?" Mom repeats. "How could you say something like that?"

"Chad."

Mom looks around at the crowd of kids and finally pieces together that Chad's not among them. Her forehead wrinkles.

"He didn't—"

"Mom," Kenzie says. "It's okay. We'll tell you everything later. Okay? Can we go home now?"

"Soon," Mom says, wiping her face. I realize then that tears have been trickling down her cheeks since I made it over the fence. "The deputies have called for a SWAT team. When they get here, the deputies will escort us back to the house if the area's been cleared. I think it has been. We'll be safe. I promise."

Her phone rings. Mom cries out as if exasperated. "Lord, what now?"

She plucks her phone out of her pocket. I notice the screen is cracked, but the phone's still working. Mom goes to her car.

Kenzie wraps an arm around me, hugging me on the side opposite Laura, who hasn't let me go.

"How do you feel?" Kenzie asks.

I can see she's trying to get me to look into her eyes, but I can't because I can't stop staring at Chad, getting cold in the November night. At the others who still swarm around the parking lot, hungry for someone to cross the fence and into their disfigured hands. At Hollis.

I look at my hands, lumps of numb flesh. Just a few minutes ago, they were washed red from my elbows to my fingertips.

"Like a monster," I say.

From the corner of my eye, I see Kenzie frown. She rests her head on my shoulder and gives me another squeeze.

"It'll pass," she says.

I turn my head toward Travis and Cammy, seated near the

patrol car. One of the cops has given them a fresh thermos, and steam rises from a Styrofoam cup they pass between them, distorting their faces, their clothes stained.

As I begin trembling uncontrollably, I look at the bodies of kids piled up in the parking lot. Black, brown, white, and all bleeding red. I wonder, suddenly, about their families, where they are, if they're safe. Jaime's little brother. Damon's mother. Travis's dad. All of them. Yesterday—god, not even twelve hours ago—I didn't care if they even *had* families.

My eyes wander along the infected students lining the fence. The ones I know, and the ones I don't. The ones I didn't want to. I shift my gaze over my shoulder and watch Mom cleaning people off while Dave passes around water bottles to the stagecraft kids. Even now, I don't know all their names.

Still studying them, I say to Kenzie, "Who are we? I mean, who are we now?"

My sister doesn't answer for a minute. Finally, she just whispers, "I love you."

I squeeze my eyes shut and try to stop shaking.

"I love you too."

We sit silently on the pavement. I want to keep my eyes closed until the sun rises. Better to imagine that for the moment, rising warm and clear over the school, over the city. Burning away the smoke and the fumes. Starting over.

Maybe someday life will somehow get back to normal. Maybe someday they can save Hollis. Maybe me and Kenzie and Laura and Cammy . . . and Travis and Serena and even

John, all of them, every last one of them, we'll all head out together. Sit on a roof like at Chad's this morning. No—no, on the ground. We'll sit together on the ground and eat cookies and microwave pizzas together.

Maybe someday . . . I'll be human.

ABOUT THE AUTHOR

Tom Leveen is the author of *Party, Zero,* and *manicpixiedreamgirl. Zero* was named to YALSA's list of Best Fiction for Young Adults. *Sick* is his first foray into the horror genre. He lives in Phoenix, Arizona.

This book was designed by Robyn Ng and art directed by Chad W. Beckerman. The text is set in 12-point Adobe Garamond, a variant of the original typeface, Garamond, created in the sixteenth century by Claude Garamond. Garamond's influences came from typfaces created and used by Venetian printers at the end of the fifteenth century. The modern version used in this book was designed by Robert Slimbach, who studied Garamond's historic typefaces at the Plantin-Moretus Museum in Antwerp, Belgium.